An
Invitation
to
Know Him
(For Yourself)

Instructor's Manual

By Mamie D. Givhan

authorHOUSE®

AuthorHouse™
1663 Liberty Drive
Bloomington, IN 47403
www.authorhouse.com
Phone: 1-800-839-8640

First published by AuthorHouse 2/16/2010

ISBN: 978-1-4490-4890-7 (e)
ISBN: 978-1-4490-4891-4 (sc)

Printed in the United States of America
Bloomington, Indiana

This book is printed on acid-free paper.

INTRODUCTION

This course consists of the first five books of the Old Testament and the first five books of the New Testament. It is set in chronological order, (by chapters and verses thereby noting the summary of events in historical order). This invitation to know Him for yourself is developed to aid you in reading your Bible, gaining insight, retaining detailed information, and defining your purpose and plans to promote the Word of God. This course corresponds with the King James Version Bible.

In reading your Bible, you will gain insight through deeper consecration by completing each blank during or after reading. This method presents a challenge to you, and by following through, personal satisfaction is accomplished.

The retaining of this information is very important—for it will not change. When you encounter any selected verse from these 10 books, regardless of how it is presented, or from any perspective, you will know the story and will magnify God even more. Following these lessons, the essays have the answers to the questions, to see that your answers coincide with the Bible.

I believe that each individual has a divine purpose and plan in his or her life; hence, *Before I formed thee in the belly, I knew thee...*(Jeremiah 1:5). Therefore, I believe you can find your divine purpose and plan through the Word of God. Stay in a good Bible-based church.

ATTENTION INSTRUCTORS: THIS MANUAL IS FOR INSTRUCTOR'S ONLY. THE ANSWERS ARE "FILLED-IN" WITH LARGER PRINT AND INCLUDES THE SCRIPTURES FOR CONFORMATION. SUGGESTIVE ESSAYS AND ANSWERS ARE LOCATED AT THE END, FOR ADDITIONAL INSIGHT.

THE OLD TESTAMENT
GENESIS

1. In the beginning GOD created the heaven and the earth. (GENESIS 1:1)

2. And the earth was without form, and void; and darkness was upon the face of the deep. AND THE SPIRIT OF GOD MOVED UPON THE FACE OF THE WATERS. (GENESIS 1:2)

3. And God called the light DAY and the darkness he called NIGHT and the evening and the morning were the FIRST DAY. (GENESIS 1:5)

4. And God called the firmament HEAVEN. And the evening and the morning were the SECOND DAY. (GENESIS 1:8)

5. And God said, let there be lights in the firmament of the heaven to divide the day from the night; AND LET THEM BE FOR SIGNS, AND FOR SEASONS AND FOR DAYS AND YEARS. (GENESIS 1:14)

6. So God created man in his own image, in the image of GOD created he him; MALE AND FEMALE CREATED HE HIM. (GENESIS 1:27)

7. On the seventh day God ended his work which he had made; and he rested on the seventh day from all his work which he had made; and he rested on the seventh day from all his work which he had made. And God BLESSED THE SEVENTH DAY AND SANCTIFIED IT: because that in it he had rested from all his work which God created and made. (GENESIS 2:2-3)

8. And the Lord God formed man of the dust of the ground, and BREATHED INTO HIS NOSTRILS THE BREATH OF LIVE AND MAN BECAME A LIVING SOUL. (GENESIS 2:7)

9. And the Lord God caused a deep sleep to fall upon Adams, and he slept: AND HE TOOK ONE OF HIS RIBS, and closed up the flesh instead thereof. And the rib, WHICH THE LORD GOD HAD TAKE FROM MAN, MADE HE A WOMAN, and brought her unto the man. And Adam said, THIS IS NOW BONE OF MY BONES AND FLESH OF MY FLESH: she shall be called woman, because she was taken out of man. Therefore shall a man leave his father and his mother and shall cleave unto his wife AND THEY SHALL BE ONE FLESH.

And they were both naked, the man and his wife, and WERE NOT ASHAMED. (GENESIS 2:21-25)

10. And the serpent said unto the woman, ye shall NOT surely die. (GENESIS 3:4)

11. And the Lord God said unto the serpent, because thou hast done this THY ART CURSED above all cattle, and above every beast of the field; UPON THY BELLY SHALL THOU GO AND DUST SHALL THOU EAT ALL THE DAYS OF THY LIFE. (GENESIS 3:14)

12. Unto Adam also and to his wife did the Lord God make coats of skins AND CLOTHED THEM. (GENESIS 3:21)

13. And Adam knew Eve his wife ; AND SHE CONCEIVED AND BARE CAIN, and said, I have gotten a man from the Lord. And she again bare his brother ABEL. Abel was a KEEPER OF SHEEP, but Cain was a TILLER OF THE GROUND. (GENESIS 4:1-2)

14. And Cain talked with Abel his brother; and it came to pass, when they were in the field, THAT CAIN ROSE UP AGAINST ABEL HIS BROTHR, AND SLEW HIM. (GENESIS 4:8)

15. And Cain said unto the Lord, MY PUNISHMENT IS GREATER THAN I CAN BEAR. (GENESIS 4:13)

16. And Cain knew his wife; and she conceived AND BARE ENOCH; and he built a city, and called the name of the city, AFTER THE NAME OF HIS SON ENOCH. (GENESIS 4:17)

17. And Adam lived an hundred and thirty years, and begat a son in his own likeness, after his image, AND CALLED HIS name SETH. (GENESIS 5:3)

18. And Lamech lived an hundred eighty and two years, AND BEGAT A SON; and he called his name NOAH, saying, this same shall comfort us concerning our work and toil of our hands BECAUSE OF THE GROUND WHICH THE LORD HATH CURSED. (GENESIS 5:28-29)

19. And Noah was five hundred years old: and Noah begat SHEM, HAM, AND JAPHETH. (GENESIS 5:32)

20. That the sons of God saw the daughters of men that they were fair; AND THEY TOOK THEM WIVES OF ALL WHICH THEY CHOSE. (GENESIS 6:2)

21. And God saw that THE WICKEDNESS OF MAN WAS GREAT IN THE EARTH, and that every imagination of the thoughts of his heart was ONLY EVIL CONTINUALLY. (GENESIS 6:5)

22. But Noah found GRACE IN THE EYES OF THE LORD. (Genesis 6:8)

23. And God said to Noah, THE END OF ALL FLESH IS COME UP BEFORE ME; for the earth is filled with violence through them, and, behold, I WILL DESTROY THEM WITH THE EARTH (GENESIS 6:13)

24. And, behold, I, even I, do BRING A FLOOD OF WATERS UPON THE EARTH to destroy all flesh, wherein is the breath of life, from under heaven AND EVERY THING THAT IS IN THE EARTH SHALL DIE. (GENESIS 6:17)

25. But with thee will I establish my covenant; AND THOU SHALL COME INTO THE ARK, thou and thy sons, and thy wife, and thy sons' wife with thee. (GENESIS 6:18)

26. Thus did Noah; according to all that God commanded him, SO DID HE. (GENESIS 6:22)

27. In the six hundredth year of Noah's life, IN THE SECOND MONTH, THE SEVENTEENTH DAY OF THE MONTH, the same day were all the fountains of the great deep broken up, and the WINDOWS OF HEAVEN WERE OPENED. And the rain was upon the earth FORTH DAYS AND FORTY NIGHTS. (GENESIS 7:11-12)

28. And the water prevailed upon the earth an HUNDRED AND FIFTY DAYS. (GENESIS 7:24)

29. And the dove came in to him in the evening; and lo, in her mouth was an olive leaf plucked off: SO NOAH KNEW THAT THE WATERS WERE ABATED FROM OFF THE EARTH. (GENESIS 8:11)

30. And the Lord smelled a sweet savour; and the Lord said in his heart, I WILL NOT AGAIN CURSE THE GROUND ANY MORE FOR MAN'S SAKE; for the imagination of man's heart is evil FROM HIS YOUTH. Neither will I again smite any more every thing living AS I HAVE DONE. (GENESIS 8:21)

31. And I will establish my covenant with you; neither shall all flesh be cut off any more by the waters of a flood; neither shall there any more be A FLOOD TO DESTROY THE EARTH. And God said THIS IS A TOKEN OF THE COVENT WHICH I MAKE BETWEEN ME AND YOU and every living creature that is with you, for perpetual generations. (GENESIS 9:11-12)

32. I do set MY BOW IN THE CLOUD and it shall be for a TOKEN OF A COVENANT BETWEEN ME AND THE EARTH. (GENESIS 9:13)

33. And he drank of the wine AND WAS DRUNKEN and he was uncovered within his tent. (GENESIS 9:21)

34. And all the days of NOAH were nine hundred and fifty years AND HE DIED. (GENESIS 9:29)

35. Now these are the generations of the sons of Noah, SHEM, HAM, AND JAPHETH; and unto them were sons born after the flood. (GENESIS 10:1)

36. And the whole earth was of ONE LANGUAGE, AND OF ONE SPEECH. (GENESIS 11:1)

37. Go to, let us go down, and there confound their language that they may NOT UNDERSTAND ONE ANOTHER'S SPEECH. (GENESIS 11:7)

38. And Terah lived seventy years, and begat ABRAM, NAHOR AND HARAN. (GENESIS 11:26)

39. And Haran DIED BEFORE HIS FATHER TERAH in the land of his nativity, in Ur of the Chaldees. (GENESIS 11:28)

40. And Abram and Nahor took them wives; THE NAME OF ABRAM'S WIFE WAS SARAI and the name of NAHOR'S WIFE, MILCAH, the daughter of Haran, the father of Milcah, and the father of Iscah. (GENESIS 11:29)

41. But Sarai WAS BARREN; she had no children. (GENESIS 11:30)

42. Now the Lord had said unto Abram, GET THEE OUT OF THY COUNTRY AND FROM THY KINDRED, AND FROM THY FATHER'S HOUSE, unto a land that I will show thee. AND I WILL MAKE THEE A GREAT NATION, AND I WILL BLESS THEE, AND MAKE THOU NAME GREAT; AND THOU SHALL BE A BLESSING. And I will bless them that bless thee, and curse him that curseth thee: AND IN THEE SHALL ALL FAMILIES OF THE EARTH BE BLESSED. So Abram departed AS THE LORD HAD SPOKEN UNTO HIM; and Lot went with him; and Abram was seventy and five years old when he departed out of Haran. (GENESIS 12:1-4)

43. Therefore it shall come to pass, when the Egyptians shall see thee, that they shall say this is his wife AND THEY WILL KILL ME, but they will save thee alive, say, I pray thee THOU ARE MY SISTER; that it may be well with me for thy sake: AND MY SOUL SHALL LIVE BECAUSE OF THEE. (GENESIS 12:12-13)

44. And Pharaoh commanded his men concerning him: AND THEY SENT HIM AWAY AND HIS WIFE, AND ALL THAT HE HAD. (GENESIS 12:20)

45. And Abram was VERY rich in cattle, and in silver, and in gold. (GENESIS (13:2)

46. And Abram said unto Lot, LET THERE BE NO STRIFE I PRAY THEE, BETWEEN ME AND THEE, and between my herdmen and thy herdmen, FOR WE BE BRETHREN. Is not the whole land before thee? Separate thyself, I pray thee, from me: IF THOU WILT TAKE THE LEFT HAND, THEN I WILL GO THE RIGHT; or if thou depart to the right hand, then I will go to the left. (GENESIS 13:8-9)

47. Then Lot chose him ALL THE PLAIN OF JORDAN. And Lot journeyed east; and they separated themselves the one from the other. Abram dwelled in THE LAND OF CANAAN, and Lot dwelled in the cities of the plain, and pitched his tent toward Sodom. (GENESIS 13:11-12)

48. For all the land which thou seest, to thee will I give it and to thy seed for ever. And I WLL MAKE THY SEED AS THE DUST OF THE EARTH, so that if a man can number the dust of the earth, then shall thy seed also be numbered. (GENESIS 13:15-16)

49. And they took Lot, Abram's brother's son, WHO DWELT IN SODOM, and his goods, and departed. (GENESIS 14:12)

50. And he brought back all the goods, AND ALSO BROUGHT AGAIN HIS BROTHER LOT, and his goods, and the women also, and the people. (GENESIS 14:16)

51. And Abram said, behold, TO ME THOU HAST GIVEN NO SEED; and lo, one born in my house is mine heir. (GENESIS 15:3)

52. And Sarai said unto Abram, behold now, THE LORD HATH RESTRAINED ME FROM BEARING; I pray thee, go in unto my maid; it may be that I may obtain children by her. And Abram hearkened to the voice of Sarai. (GENESIS 16:2)

53. And he went in unto Hagar, AND SHE CONCEIVED, and when she saw that she had conceived, HER MISTRESS WAS DESPISED IN HER EYES. (GENESIS 16:4)

54. And the Angel of the Lord found her BY A FOUNTAIN OF WATER, in the wilderness, by the fountain in the way to Shur. (GENESIS 16:7)

55. And the Angel of the Lord said unto her, I WILL MULTIPLY THOU SEED EXCEEDINGLY, that it shall not be NUMBERED for multitude. And the Angel of the Lord said unto her, behold, thy art with child, and shall bare a son, and shall call his name ISHMAEL because the Lord hath heard thy affliction. (Genesis 16:10-11)

56. And Hagar bare Abram a son and Abram called his son's name, WHICH HAGAR BARE, ISHMAEL. (GENESIS 16:15)

57. Neither shall thy name any more be called ABRAM, but thy name shall be ABRAHAM; for a father of many nations have I made thee. (GENESIS 17:5)

58. This is my covenant, which ye shall keep, between me and you and thy seed after thee; EVERY MAN CHILD AMOUNG YOU SHALL BE CIRCUMCISED. And ye shall circumcise the flesh of your foreskin; and it shall be A TOKEN OF THE COVENANT BETWIXT ME AND YOU.(GENESIS 17:10-11)

59. And God said unto Abraham, AS FOR SARAI thy wife, thou shall not call her name Sarai, BUT SARAH SHALL BE HER NAME. (GENESIS 17:15)

60. And God said, Sarah thy wife shall BEAR THEE A SON INDEED AND THOU SHALL CALL HIS NAME ISAAC; and I will establish my covenant with him for an everlasting covenant, and with his seed after him. And as for ISHMAEL, I have heard thee; behold, I HAVE BLESSED HIM, and will make him fruitful, and will multiply him exceedingly; TWELVE PRINCES SHALL HE BEGET, and I will make him a great nation. (GENESIS 17:19-20)

61. And all the men of his house, born in the house, and bought with money of the stranger, WERE CIRCUMCISED WITH HIM. (GENESIS 17:27)

62. And Abraham drew near, and said, wilt thou also destroy THE RIGHTEOUS WITH THE WICKED? (GENESIS 18:23)

63. And the Lord said, if I find IN SODOM FIFTY RIGHTEOUS WITHIN THE CITY, then I will spare ALL THE PLACE FOR THEIR SAKES. (GENESIS 18:26)

64. And it came to pass, when they had brought them forth abroad, that he said, escape for thy life; LOOK NOT BEHIND THEE, neither stay thou in all the plain; escape to the mountain, lest THOU BE CONSUMED. (GENESIS 19:17)

65. Then the Lord rained UPON SODOM AND UPON GOMORAH BRIMSTONE AND FIRE from the Lord out of Heaven. (GENESIS 19:24)

66. But his wife LOOKED BACK from behind him, and she BECAME A PILLAR OF SALT. (GENESIS 19:26)

67. And the firstborn said unto the younger, OUR FATHER IS OLD and there is not a man in the earth TO COME IN UNTO US after the manner of all the earth. (GENESIS 19:31)

68. Thus were both the DAUGHTERS OF LOT WITH CHILD BY THEIR FATHER. And the firstborn bare a son, and called his name MOAB; the same is the father of the MOABITS unto this day. And the younger, she bare a son, and called his name BEN-AMMI; the same is the father of the children of AMMON UNTO THIS DAY.(GENESIS 19:36-38)

69. And yet indeed she is my sister; SHE IS THE DAUGHTER OF MY FATHER, BUT NOT THE DAUGHTER OF MY MOTHER and she became my wife. (GENESIS 20:12)

70. For Sarah conceived and bare Abraham a son in his old age, at the set time of which God had spoken to him. And Abraham called the name of his son that was born unto him, WHOM SARAH BARE TO HIM ISAAC.(GENESIS 21:2-3)

71. And Abraham rose up early in the morning, AND TOOK BREAD, AND A BOTTLE OF WATER, and gave it unto HAGAR, putting it on her shoulder, and the child, and sent her away, and she departed and wandered in the wilderness of BEER-SHEBA. (GENESIS 21:14)

72. Arise, lift up the lad, and hold him in thine hand; FOR I WILL MAKE HIM A GREAT NATION. (GENESIS 21:18)

73. And Abraham reproved Abimelech BECAUSE OF A WELL OF WATER, which Abimelech's servants had violently taken away. (GENESIS 21:25)

74. And Abraham took sheep and oxen, and gave them unto Abimelech; AND BOTH OF THEM MADE A COVENENAT. (GENESIS 21:27)

75. And he said, for these seven ewe lambs, THOU SHALL TAKE MY HAND that they may be a WITNESS UNTO ME, that I have digged this well (GENESIS 21:30).

76. And Abraham stretched forth his hand, and took the knife TO SLAY HIS SON. (GENESIS 22:10)

77. And Abraham lifted up his eyes, and looked, and behold, BEHIND HIM A RAM CAUGHT IN THE THICKET BY HIS HORNS; and Abraham went and took the ram, and offered him up for a brunt offering IN THE STEAD OF HIS SON. (GENESIS 22:13)

78. That in blessing I will bless thee, and in multiplying I will multiply thy seed as the STARS OF THE HEAVEN, AND AS THE SAND WHICH IS UPON THE SEA SHORE; and thy seed shall possess the gate of his enemies. And in thy seed shall all the nations of the earth be blessed; BECAUSE THOU HAST OBEYED MY VOICE. (GENESIS 22:17-18)

79. And Sarah was an hundred and seven and twenty years old; these were the years of THE LIFE OF SARAH. (GENESIS 23:1)

80. My lord, hearken unto me; THE LAND IS WORTH FOUR HUNDRED SHEKELS OF SILVER; ; What is that betwixt me and thee? Bury therefore, thy dead. (GENESIS 23:15)

81. And after this, Abraham buried Sarah his wife in the cave of the FIELD OF MACHPELAH BEFORE MAMRE; the same is Hebron in the land of Canaan. (GENESIS 23:19)

82. And the field, and the cave that is therein, were made sure UNTO ABRAHAM for a possession of a burying place BY THE SONS OF HETH. (GENESIS 23:20)

83. But thou shalt go unto my country, and to my kindred, and TAKE A WIFE UNTO MY SON ISAAC. (GENESIS 24:4)

84. And it came to pass, before he had done speaking, that, behold, REBEKAH CAME OUT, who was born to Bethuel, son of Milcah, the wife of Nahor, Abraham's brother, WITH A PITCHER UPON HER SHOULDER. (GENESIS 24:15)

85. Behold, Rebekah is before thee, TAKE HER AND GO, and let her be thy master's son's wife, as the Lord hath spoken. (GENESIS 24:51)

86. Then again Abraham took a wife, AND HER NAME WAS KETURAH. And she bare him ZIMRAN, and JOKSHAN, and MEDAN, and MIDIAN, And ISHBAK, and SHUAH. (GENESIS 25:1-2)

87. And Abraham gave all that HE HAD UNTO ISAAC. (GENESIS 25:5)

88. And these are the days of the years of Abraham's life which he lived, AN HUNDRED THREESCORE AND FIFTEEN YEARS. (GENESIS 25:7)

89. And his sons ISAAC AND ISHMAEL buried him in the cave of Machpelah, in the field of Ephron the son of Zohar the Hattlte, WHICH IS BEFORE MAMRE. (GENESIS 25:9)

90. The field which Abraham purchased of the sons of Heth; THERE WAS ABRAHAM BURIED AND SARAH HIS WIFE. (GENESIS 25:10)

91. And the Lord said unto her, TWO NATIONS ARE IN THY WOMB and two manner of people shall be separated from thy bowels; and the one people shall be stronger than the other people, AND THE ELDER SHALL SERVE THE YOUNGER. And when her days to be delivered were fulfilled, behold, there were TWINS IN HER WOMB. And the first COME OUT RED ALL OVER, LIKE A HAIRY GARMENT; and they call his name ESAU. And after that came his brother out, and HIS HAND TOOK HOLD OF ESAU'S HEEL; and his name was called JACOB: and Isaac was threescore years old when she bare them. And the boys grew; and ESAU was a cunning hunter, a man of the field; and JACOB was a plain man, dwelling in tents . (GENESIS 25:23-27)

92. And Isaac loved Esau, because he did eat of his venison; BUT REBEKAH LOVED JACOB. (GENESIS 25:28)

93. And Jacob said swear to me this day; and he sware unto him and HE SOLD HIS BIRTHRIGHTS UNTO JACOB. (GENESIS 25:33)

94. Because that Abraham obeyed my voice and kept my charge, MY COMMANDMENTS, MY STATUTES AND MY LAWS. (GENESIS 26:5)

95. And Isaac digged again the wells of water, which they had digged in the day of Abraham his father; FOR THE PHILISTINES HAD STOPPED THEM AFTER THE DEATH OF ABRAHAM; and he called their names after the names by which his father had called them. (GENESIS 26:18)

96. And the Lord appeared unto him the same night, and said, I AM THE GOD OF ABRAHAM THY FATHER; FEAR NOT FOR I AM WITH THEE AND WILL BLESS THEE, and multiply thy seed for my servant Abraham's sake. (GENESIS 26:24)

97. And they rose up betimes in the morning , and SWARE ONE TO ANOTHER; and Isaac sent them away and they DEPARTED FROM HIM IN PEACE. (GENESIS 26:31).

98. And it came to pass, that when Isaac was old, and his eyes were dim, so that he could not see, HE CALLED ESAU HIS ELDEST SON, and said unto him, my son, and he said unto him, behold, here am I. (GENESIS 27:1)

99. And make me savory meat such as I love, and bring it to me, that I may eat; THAT MY SOUL MAY BLESS THEE BEFORE I DIE . (GENESIS 27:4)

100.   And Jacob said to Rebekah his mother, behold, Esau my brother IS A HAIRY MAN, AND I AM A SMOOTH MAN. (GENESIS 27:11)

101.   And she put the skins of the kids of the goat UPON HIS HANDS, AND UPON THE SMOOTH OF HIS NECK. (GENESIS 27:16)

102.   And Jacob went near unto Isaac his father; and he felt him, and said THE VOICE OF JACOB'S , BUT THE HANDS ARE THE HANDS OF ESAU . And he discerned him not, because his hands were hairy, as his brother Esau's hands : SO HE BLESSED HIM.   And he said, art thou my very son Esau? And he said, I AM. (GENESIS 27:22-24)

103.   And it came to pass, as soon as Isaac had made an end of blessing Jacob, and Jacob was yet scarce gone out from the present of Isaac his father, THAT ESAU HIS BROTHER CAME IN FROM HIS HUNTING. (GENESIS 27:30)

104.   And he said, thy brother came with subtlety, AND HATH TAKEN AWAY THY BLESSING. (GENESIS 2735)

105.   And he said, is not he rightly named Jacob? For he hath supplanted me these two times: HE TOOK AWAY MY BIRTHRIGHT, AND BEHOLD, NOW HE HAST TAKEN AWAY MY BLESSING and he said, hast thou not reserved a blessing for me? (GENESIS 27:36)

106.   And Esau hated Jacob because of the blessing wherewith his father blessed him; and Esau said in his heart, the days of mourning for my father are at hand; THEN WILL I SLAY MY BROTHER JACOB. (GENESIS 27:41)

107.   And he dreamed, and behold a ladder set up on the earth, AND THE TOP OF IT REACHED TO HEAVEN and behold the angel of God ascending and descending on it. (GENESIS 28:12)

108.   And this stone, which I have set for a pillar, shall be GOD'S HOUSE: and of all that THOU SHALT GIVE ME I WILL SURELY GIVE THE TENTH UNTO THEE. (GENESIS 28:22)

109. And he said unto them, is he well? And they said, he is well, and BEHOLD, RACHAEL HIS DAUGHTER COMETH with the sheep. (GENESIS 29:6)

110. And Laban had two daughters the name of the ELDER WAS LEAH and the name of the YOUNGER WAS RACHEL. (GENESIS 29:16)

111. And Jacob loved Rachel; and said, I WILL SERVE THEE SEVEN YEARS FOR RACHEL, thy younger daughter. (GENESIS 29:18)

112. And it came to pass in the evening THAT HE TOOK LEAH his daughter and brought her to him AND HE WENT IN UNTO HER. (GENESIS 29:23)

113. And Jacob did so, and fulfilled her week AND HE GAVE HIM RACHEL HIS DAUGHTER TO WIFE ALSO. (GENESIS 29:28)

114. And Leah conceived, and bare a son, and she called his name REUBEN for she said, surely the Lord hath LOOKED UPON MY AFFLICTION, now therefore my husband will love me. (GENESIS 29:32)

115. When Leah saw that she had left bearing, SHE TOOK ZILPAH HER MAID, AND GAVE HER JACOB TO WIFE. (GENESIS 30:9)

116. And it came to pass, when RACHEL HAD BORN JOSEPH that Jacob said unto Laban, send me away, that I may go unto MINE OWN PLACE and to my country. (GENESIS 30:25)

117. And the flocks conceived before THE ROD and brought forth cattle, RINGSTRAKED, SPECKLED, AND SPOTTED. (GENESIS 30:39)

118. And the man INCREASE EXCEEDINGLY and had much cattle, and maidservants, and menservants and camels, and asses. (GENESIS 30:43)

119. And the Lord said unto Jacob, return unto the land of thy fathers, and to thy kindred, AND I WILL BE WITH THEE. (GENESIS 31:3)

120. And the angel of God spake unto me in a dream, saying JACOB; and I said, here am I. and he said, lift up now thine eyes, and see all the RAMS WHICH LEAP UPON THE CATTLE ARE RINGSTRAKE, SPECKLED AND GRISLED; for I have seen all that LABAN doeth unto thee. I AM THE GOD OF BETH-EL , where thou anointest the pillar and where thou VOWEDST A VOW UNTO ME; now arise, get thee out from this land, and return unto the land of thy kindred. (GENESIS 31:11-13)

121. And Jacob stole away UNAWARES TO LABAN THE SYRIAN in that he told him not that he fled. (GENESIS 31:20)

122. And God came to Laban the Syrian in a dream by night and said unto him, TAKE HEED THAT THOUS SPEAK NOT TO JACOB EITHER GOOD OR BAD. (GENESIIS 31:24)

123. And Jacob answered and said to Laban, BECAUSE I WAS AFRAID; for I said peradventure thou wouldest TAKE BY FORCE THY DAUGHTERS FROM ME. (GENESIS 31:31)

124. Thus have I been twenty years in thy house; I SERVED THEE FOURTEEN YEARS FOR THY DAUGHTERS, and six years for thy cattle and thou hast changed my wages ten times. (GENESIS 31:41)

125. Now therefore come thou let us MAKE A COVENANT, I AND THOU; and let it be for a witness between me and thee. (GENESIS 31:44)

126. And Mizpah; for he said, the Lord watch between me and thee, WHEN WE ARE ABSENT, ONE FROM ANOTHER. (GENESIS 31:49)

127. This heap be witness, and this pillar be witness, that I WILL NOT PASS OVER THIS HEAP TO THEE and that thou SHALL NOT PASS OVER THIS HEAP and this pillar unto me FOR HARM. (GENESIS 31:52)

128. And Jacob sent messengers before him ESAU HIS BROTHER unto the land of Seir, the country of Edom. (GENESIS 32:3)

129. And said, if Esau come to the one company, and smite it, then THE OTHER COMPANY WHICH IS LEFT SHALL ESCAPE. (GENESIS 32:8)

130. And Jacob was left alone; and there WRESTLED A MAN WITH HIM UNTIL THE BREAKING OF THE DAY. (GENESIS 32:24)

131. And he said, let me go, for the day breaketh. And he said, I WILL NOT LET THEE GO, EXCEPT THOU BLESS ME. (GENESIS 32:26)

132. And he said, thy name shall be called no more, Jacob, BUT ISRAEL for as a prince hast thou power with God and with men and hast prevailed. (GENESIS 32:28)

133. And Jacob called the name of the place Peniel; FOR I HAVE SEEN GOD FACE TO FACE, and my life is preserved. (GENESIS 32:30)

134. And Esau RAN TO MEET HIM, and embraced him, and fell on his neck, and kissed him AND THEY WEPT. (GENESIS 33:4)

135. But in this will we consent unto you; if ye will be as we be, THAT EVERY MALE OF YOU BE CIRCUMCISED. (GENESIS 34:15)

136. And it came to pass on the third day, when they were sore, that two of the sons of Jacob, SIMEON AND LEVI , Dinah's brethren, took each man his sword AND CAME UPON THE CITY BOLDLY AND SLEW ALL THE MALES. (GENESIS 34:25)

137. And God said unto Jacob, arise, go up to Beth-el and dwell there; and make there an altar unto God, that appeared unto thee WHEN THOU FLEDDEST FROM THE FACE OF ESAU THY BOTHER. (GENESIS 35:1)

138. And God said unto him, thy name is Jacob; thy name shall not be called any more Jacob, BUT ISRAEL SHALL BE THY NAME; and he called his name Israel. And God said unto him I AM God Almighty; be fruitful and multiply; A NATION AND A COMPANY OF NATIONS shall be of thee, and Kings shall come out of thy loins. (GENESIS 35:10-11)

139. And God went up from him in the place WHERE HE TALKED WITH HIM. (GENESIS 35:13)

140. And it came to pass as her soul was departing (for she died) that she called his name Ben-oni BUT HIS FATHER CALL HIM BENJAMIN. (GENESIS 35:18)

141. And Jacob set a pillar upon her grave; THAT IS THE PILLAR OF RACHEL'S GRAVE unto this day. (GENESIS 35:20)

142. And it came to pass, when Israel dwelt in that land, that Ruben went and lay with Bilhah his FATHER'S CONCUBINE; and Israel heard it. NOW THE SONS OF JACOB WERE TWELVE. (GENESIS 35:22)

143. The sons of Leah: REUBEN, Jacob's firstborn and SIMEON and LEVI and JUDAH and ISSACHAR and ZEBULUM . (GENESIS 35:23)

144. The sons of Rachel; JOSEPH and BENJAMIN. (GENESIS 35:24)

145. And the sons of Bilhah Rachel's handmaid DAN and NAPHTALI. (GENESIS 35:25)

146. And the sons of Zilpah, Leah's handmaind; GAD and ASHER ; these are the sons of Jacob, which were born to him in Padan-aram. (GENESIS 35:26)

147. And the days of Isaac were an hundred and fourscores years. And ISAAC GAVE UP THE GHOST AND DIED, and was gathered unto his people, being old and full of days; and his sons ESAU and JACOB BURIED HIM. (GENESIS 35:28-29)

148. Now these are the generations of Esau, WHO IS EDOM. (GENESIS 36:1)

149. And these are the names of the dukes that came of Esau, according to their families, after their places, by their names: duke TIMNAH, duke ALVAN, duke JETHETH (GENESIS 36:40)

150. Now Israel loved Joseph MORE THAN ALL HIS CHILDREN, because he was the son of his old age AND HE MADE HIM A COAT OF MANY COLOURS. (GENESIS 37:3)

151. And Joseph dreamed a dream, and he told it his brethren; AND THEY HATED HIM YET THE MORE (GENESIS 37:5)

152. And they said one to another BEHOLD, THIS DREAMER COMETH. (GENESIS 37:19)

153. And Ruben heard it, and he delivered him out of their hands and said, LET US NOT KILL HIM. (GENESIS 37:21)

154. And it came to pass, when Joseph was come unto his brethren that they stripped Joseph out of his coat, HIS COAT OF MANY COLOURS that was on him, and they took him, and cast him into a pit, AND THE PIT WAS EMPTY, there was no water in it. (GENESIS 37:23-24)

155. Then there passed by Midianites merchantmen; and they drew and lifted up Joseph out of the pit, AND SOLD JOSEPH TO THE ISHMEELITES FOR TWENTY PIECES OF SILVER; and they brought Joseph into EGYPT. (GENESIS 37:28)

156. And Jacob rent his clothes, and put sackcloth upon his loin, AND MOURNED FOR HIS SON MANY DAYS. (GENESIS 37:34)

157.	And Judah acknowledged them, and said, SHE HAD BEEN MORE RIGHTEOUS THAN THOU: because that I gave her not to Shelan my son. And he knew her no more. (GENESIS 38:26)

158.	And it came to pass in the time of her travail, that BEHOLD, TWINS WERE IN HER WOMB (GENSIS 38:27)

159.	And Joseph found grace in his sight, and he served him, and HE MADE HIM OVERSEER OVER HIS HOUSE, and all that he had he put into his hand. (GENESIS 39:4)

160.	And it came to pass after these things, that his master's WIFE CAST HER EYES UPON JOSEPH and she said LIE WITH HIM. (GENESIS 39:7)

161.	There is none greater in this house than I; neither hath he kept back anything from me but thee, because thou art his wife; HOW THEN CAN I DO THIS GREAT WICKEDNESS, AND SIN AGAINST GOD? (GENESIS 39:9)

162.	And she caught him by his garment, saying, LIE WITH ME; and he left his garment in her hand, and fled and got him out. (GENESIS 39:12)

163.	And it came to pass, when his master heard the WORDS OF HIS WIFE, which she spake unto him, saying, after this manner did thy servant to me ; THAT HIS WRATH WAS KINDLED. And Joseph's master took him AND PUT HIM INTO THE PRISON, a place where the king's prisoners were bond; and he was there in the prison. But the Lord was with Joseph, and showed him mercy, AND GAVE HIM FAVOUR IN THE SIGHT OF THE KEEPER OF THE PRISON. (GENESIS 39:19-21)

164.	And they dreamed a dream both of them, EACH MAN HIS DREAM IN ONE NIGHT, each man according to the interpretation of his dream, THE BUTLER AND THE BAKER of the king of Egypt, which were bound in the prison. (GENESIS 40:5)

165.	And Joseph said unto him, this is the interpretation of it: THE THREE BRANCHES ARE THREE DAYS; yet within three days shall Pharaoh lift up thine head, AND RESTORE THEE UNTO THY PLACE and thou shall deliver

Pharaoh's cup into his hand, after the former manner when thou wast his bulter. (GENESIS 40:12-13)

166. And Joseph answered and said, this is the interpretation thereof; THE THREE BASKETS ARE THREE DAYS; yet within three days shall Pharaoh lift up thy head from off thee, AND SHALL HANG THEE ON A TREE and the birds shall eat thy flesh from off thee. (GENESIS 40:18-19)

167. And he restored the chief butler UNTO HIS BUTLERSHIP AGAIN and he gave the cup into Pharaoh's hand. But he HANGED THE CHIEF BAKER as Joseph had interpreted to them. Yet did not the CHIEF BUTLER remember Joseph, BUT FORGOT HIM. (GENESIS 40:21-23)

168. And Joseph said unto Pharaoh, the dream of Pharaoh is ONE; God hath shown Pharaoh what he is about to do. The SEVEN GOOD KINE are SEVEN YEARS; and the SEVEN GOOD EARS are SEVEN YEARS; THE DREAM IS ONE. (GENESIS 41:25-26)

169. And in the seven plenteous years THE EARTH BROUGHT FORTH BY HANDFULS. (GENESIS 41:47)

170. And the seven years of plenteousness, that was in the land of Egypt, WERE ENDED. And the seven years of dearth began to come ACCORDING AS JOSEPH HAD SAID; and the dearth was in all lands BUT IN ALL THE LAND OF EGYPT THERE WERE BREAD. (GENESIS 41:53-54)

171. And all countries came into Egypt to JOSEPH TO BUY CORN because that the famine was so sore in all lands. (GENESIS 41:57)

172. Now when Jacob saw that there was corn in Egypt, Jacob said unto his sons, WHY DO YE LOOK ONE UPON ANOTHER? (GENESIS 42:1)

173. And Joseph's TEN BROTHERS went down to buy corn in Egypt. (GENESIS 42:3)

174. And Joseph saw his brethren AND HE KNEW THEM, but made himself strange unto them, and spake roughly unto them, and he said unto them, whence come ye? And they said, FROM THE LAND OF CANAAN to buy corn. (GENESIS 42:7)

175. Hereby ye shall be PROVED; by the life of Pharaoh ye shall not go forth, EXCEPT YOUR YOUNGEST BROTHER COME HITHER. (GENESIS 42:15)

176. And they knew not that Joseph understood them FOR HE SPAKE UNTO THEM BY AN INTERPRETER. (GENESIS 42:23)

177. And we said unto him, we are true men; WE ARE NO SPIES. (GENESIS 42:31)

178. We be twelve brethren, sons of our father; ONE IS NOT, and the youngest is this day with our father IN THE LAND OF CANAAN. (GENESIS 42:32)

179. And the men took that PRESENT, and they took DOUBLE MONEY in their hand, and BENJAMIN and rose up, and went down to Egypt and stood before Joseph. (GENESIS 43:15)

180. And when Joseph saw Benjamin with them, he said to the ruler of his house, BRING THESE MEN HOME, AND SLAY, AND MAKE READY; FOR THESE MEN SHALL DINE WITH ME AT NOON. (GENESIS 43:16)

181. And Joseph made haste for his bowels did yearn upon his brother; and he sought where to weep; AND HE ENTERED INTO HIS CHAMBERS, AND WEPT THERE. (GENESIS 43:30)

182. And the one went out from me, and I said surely he is torn in pieces, AND I SAW HIM NOT SINCE. (GENESIS 44:28)

183. And Joseph said unto his brethren, COME NEAR TO ME, I pray you. And they came near, and he said, I AM JOSEPH YOUR BROTHER, WHOM YE SOLD INTO EGYPT. (GENESIS 45:4)

184. And they told him all the words of Joseph, which he had said unto them; and when he saw the wagons which Joseph had sent to carry him, THE SPIRIT OF JACOB THEIR FATHER REVIVED. And Israel said, it is enough; Joseph my son is yet alive; I WILL GO AND SEE HIM BEFORE I DIE. (GENESIS 45:27-28)

185. And Jacob rose up from Beer-Sheba AND THE SONS OF ISRAEL CARRIED JACOB THEIR FATHER, and their little ones, and their wives in the wagons which Pharaoh had sent to carry him. (GENESIS 46:5)

186. And Joseph made ready his chariot, and went up to meet ISRAEL HIS FATHER to Goshen, and presented himself unto him AND HE FELL ON HIS NECK AND WEPT ON HIS NECK A GOOD WHILE. And Israel said unto Joseph, NOW LET ME DIE, SINCE I HAVE SEEN THY FACE, because thou art yet alive. (GENESIS 46:29-30)

187. And Joseph brought all the LAND OF EGYPT FOR PHARAOH for the Egyptians sold every man his field, because the famine prevailed over them: SO THE LAND BECAME PHARAOH'S. (GENESIS 47:20)

188. And Jacob lived in the land of Egypt SEVENTEEN YEARS so the whole age of Jacob was an hundred forty and seven years. (GENESIS 47:28)

189. But I will lie with my fathers AND THOU SHALL CARRY ME OUT OF EGYPT AND BURY ME IN THEIR BURYINGPLACE. And he said, I will do as thou hast said. (GENESIS 47:30)

190. And his father refused, and said I KNOW IT MY SON, I KNOW IT; he also shall be great; BUT TRULY HIS YOUNGER BROTHER SHALL BE GREATER THAN HE and his seed shall become A MULTITUDE OF NATIONS. (GENESIS 48:19)

191. And Jacob called unto his sons, and said, GATHER YOURSELVES TOGETHER, that I may tell you that which shall befall you in the last days. Gather yourselves together AND HEAR, YE SONS OF JACOB AND HEARKEN UNTO ISRAEL YOUR FATHER. (GENESIS 49:1-2)

192. All these are the TWELVE TRIBES OF ISRAEL, and this is it that their father spake unto them and blessed them; EVERY ONE ACCORDING TO HIS BLESSING, HE BLESSED THEM. (GENESIS 49:28)

193. And he charged them, and said unto them, I am to be gathered unto my people BURY ME WITH MY FATHER IN THE CAVE THAT IS IN THE FIELD OF EPHRON THE HITTITE. In the cave that is in the FIELD OF MACHPELAH, which is before Mamre, IN THE LAND OF CANAAN which ABRAHAM bought with the field Ephron the Hittite for a possession OF A BURYING-PLEACE. There they buried ABRAHAM and SARAH his wife; there they buried ISAAC and REBEHAK his wife and there I buried LEAH. The purchase of the field and of the cave that is therein as FROM THE CHILDREN OF HETH. And when Jacob had made an end of commanding his

sons, he gathered up his feet into the bed and YIELDED UP THE GHOST, AND WAS GATHERED UNTO HIS PEOPLE. (GENESIS 49:29-33)

194. And Joseph fell upon his father's face, and WEPT UPON HIM AND KISS HIM. And Joseph commanded his servants the physicians to EMBALM HIS FATHER; AND THE PHYSICIANS EMBALMED ISRAEL. (GENESIS 50:1-2)

195. And Pharaoh said, go up, and bury thy father, ACCORDING AS HE MADE THEE SWEAR. (GENESIS 50:6)

196. And there went up with him both chariots and horsemen: AND IT WAS A VERY GREAT COMPANY. (GENESIS 50:9)

197. And his sons did unto him according as he commanded them; for his sons carried him INTO THE LAND OF CANAAN AND BURIED HIM, in the cave of the field of Machpelah, which ABRAHAM bought with the field for a possession of a burying place of Ephron the Hattite, before MAMRE (GENESIS 50:12-13)

198. So shall we say unto Joseph, forgive, I pray thee now, THE TRESPASS OF THY BRETHREN, AND THEIR SINS; for they did unto thee evil; and now, we pray thee, forgive the trespass of the servants of the God of thy father. AND JOSEPH WEPT WHEN THEY SPAKE UNTO HIM. (GENESIS 50:17)

199. But as for you ye thought evil against me; BUT GOD MEANT IT UNTO GOOD, to bring to pass, as it is this day. (GENESIS 50:20)

200. And Joseph said unto his brethren, I die; and God will surely visit you, and bring you out of this land unto the land which he sware TO ABRAHAM, TO ISAAC AND TO JACOB. (GENESIS 50:24)

201. And Joseph took an oath of THE CHILDREN OF ISRAEL, saying, God will surely visit you, AND YE SHALL CARRY UP MY BONES FROM HENCE. So Joseph died, being an hundred and ten years old; and they embalmed him, and he was put in a coffin in EGYPT. (GENESIS 50:25-26)

THE END GENESIS

EXODUS

1. Now these are the names of the CHILDREN OF ISRAEL, which came into Egypt; every man and his household came with JACOB. (EXODUS 1:1)

2. And Joseph died, and all his brethren, AND ALL THAT GENERATION. (EXODUS 1:6)

3. And he said unto his people, behold, the people of the children of Israel ARE MORE AND MIGHTIER THAN WE. (EXODUS 1:9)

1. 4. And the Egyptians made THE CHILDREN OF ISRAEL to serve with rigour. (EXODUS 1:13)

5. And Pharaoh charged all his people, saying, EVERY SON THAT IS BORN YE SHALL CAST INTO THE RIVER, and every daughter ye shall save alive. (EXODUS 1:22)

6. And when she had opened it SHE SAW THE CHILD and behold, THE BABY WEPT and she had compassion on him, and said this is one of THE HEBREWS' CHILDREN. (EXODUS 2:6)

7. And the child grew, and she brought him unto PHARAOH'S DAUGHTER AND HE BECAME HER SON. And she called his name MOSES; and she said, BECAUSE I DREW HIM OUT OF THE WATER. (EXODUS 2:10)

8. And he looked this way and that way and when he saw that there was no man, HE SLEW THE EGYPTIAN AND HID HIM IN THE SAND. (EXODUS 2:12)

9. Now when Pharaoh heard this thing, HE SOUGHT TO SLAY MOSES. But Moses fled FROM THE FACE OF PHARAOH and dwelt in the land of Midian: and sat down by a well. (EXODUS 2:15)

10. And Moses was content to dwell with the man: AND HE GAVE MOSES ZIPPORAH HIS DAUGHTER. And she bare him a son, and he called his name GERSHON for he said, I have been a stranger in A STRANGE LAND. (EXODUS 2:21-22)

11. And God heard their groaning and God remembered his Covenant with ABRAHAM, WITH ISAAC AND WITH JACOB. (EXODUS 2:24)

12. Now Moses kept the flock of Jethro his father-in-law, the priest of Midian: AND HE LED THE FLOCK TO THE BACKSIDE OF THE DESERT, and came to the mountain of God, even to Horeb. (EXODUS 3:1)

13. And Moses said, I will now turn aside, and see this great sight, WHY THE BUSH IS NOT BURNT . (EXODUS 3:3)

14. And he said, draw not nigh hither: PUT OFF THY SHOES FROM OFF THY FEET, FOR THE PLACE WHEREON THY STANDEST IS HOLY GROUND. (EXODUS 3:5)

15. Come now therefore, and I will send thee unto Pharaoh, that thou mayest BRING FORTH MY PEOPLE THE CHILDREN OF ISRAEL OUT OF EGYPT. (EXODUS 3:10)

16. And God said unto Moses I AM THAT I AM. And he said, thus shalt thou say unto the children of Israel I AM HATH SENT ME UNTO YOU. (EXODUS 3:14)

17. Go and gather the elders of Israel together, and say unto them, the Lord God of Abraham, of Isaac, and of Jacob appeared unto me, saying, I HAVE SURELY VISITED YOU AND SEEN THAT WHICH IS DONE TO YOU IN EGYPT. And I have said, I WILL BRING YOU UP OUT OF THE AFFICTION OF EGYPT unto the land of Canaanites, and the Hittites and the Amorites, and the Perizzites, and the Hivites, and the Jebusites, UNTO A LAND FLOWING WITH MILD LAND HONEY. (EXODUS 3:16-17)

18. And I will stretch out my hand, and smite Egypt WITH ALL MY WONDERS which I will do in the midst thereof; and AFTER THAT HE WILL LET YOU GO. (EXODUS 3:20)

19. And the Lord said unto him, what is that in thine hand? And he said, A ROD. (EXODUS 4:2)

20. And Moses said unto the Lord, O my Lord, I AM NOT ELOQUENT, neither heretofore, nor since thou hast spoken unto thy servant: BUT I AM SLOW OF SPEECH, AND OF A SLOW TONGUE. (EXODUS 4:10)

21. Now therefore go, and I will be with thy MOUTH, AND TEACH THEE WHAT THOU SHALL SAY. (EXODUS 4:12)

22. And the anger of the Lord was kindled against Moses, and he said, IS NOT AARON THE LEVITE THY BROTHER? I KNOW THAT HE CAN SPEAK WELL. And also, behold, he cometh forth to meet thee: and when he seeth thee HE WILL BE GLAD IN HIS HEART. (EXODUS 4:14)

23. And he shall be thy SPOKESMAN UNTO THE PEOPLE: and he shall be, even he shall be to thee instead of a mouth, and THOU SHALT BE TO HIM INSTEAD OF GOD. (EXODUS 4:16)

24. And Moses took his wife and his son, and set them upon an ass AND RETURNED TO THE LAND OF EGYPT; and Moses took THE ROD OF GOD IN HIS HAND. (EXODUS 4:20)

25. And Aaron spoke all the words WHICH THE LORD HAD SPOKEN UNTO MOSES, and did the signs in the sight of the people. (EXODUS 4:30)

26. And afterward Moses and Aaron went in, and told Pharaoh, thus saith the Lord God of Israel, LET MY PEOPLE GO, that they may hold a feast unto me in the wilderness. And Pharaoh said, who is the Lord, THAT I SHOULD OBEY HIS VOICE TO LET ISRAEL GO? I know not the Lord, NEITHER WILL I LET ISRAEL GO. (EXODUS 5:1-2)

27. For since I came to Pharaoh to speak in thy name, he hath done evil to this people, NEITHER HAST THOU DELIVERED THY PEOPLE AT ALL. (EXODUS 5:23)

28. And God spake unto Moses and said unto him I AM THE LORD. And I appeared unto Abraham, unto Isaac, and unto Jacob, by the name of GOD ALMIGHTY but by my name JEHOVAH WAS I NOT KNOWN TO THEM, and I have also established a COVENANT with them to give them the land of Canaan, the land of their pilgrimage, WHEREIN THEY WERE STRANGERS. (EXODUS 6:2-4)

29. And the Lord said unto Moses, see, I have made thee a god to Pharaoh: AND AARON THY BROTHER SHALL BE THY PROPHET. (EXODUS 7:1)

30. And Moses and Aaron went in unto Pharaoh, and they did so as the Lord had commanded: and Aaron cast down his rod before Pharaoh, and before his servants, AND IT BECAME A SERPENT. (EXODUS 7:10)

31. For they cast down every man his rod, and they became serpents but AARON'S ROD SWALLOWED UP THEIR RODS. (EXODUS 7:12)

32. And Moses and Aaron did so, as the Lord commanded; and he lifted up the rod, and smote the waters that were in the river, IN THE SIGHT OF PHARAOH, and in the sight of his servants, AND ALL THE WATER THAT WERE IN THE RIVER WERE TURNED TO BLOOD. (EXODUS 7:20)

33. And the Lord spake unto Moses , say unto Aaron, STRECTH FORTH THINE HAND WITH THY ROD over the streams, over the rivers and over the ponds and CAUSE FROGS TO COME UP UPON THE LAND OF EGYPT. (EXODUS 8:5)

34. And the Lord said unto Moses, say unto Aaron, stretch out thy rod and smite the dust of the land, THAT IT MAY BECOME LICE THROUGHOUT ALL THE LAND OF EGYPT. (EXODUS 8:16)

35. And the Lord did so; and THERE CAME A GRIEVOUS SWARM OF FLIES into the house of Pharaoh, and into his servants' houses and into all the land of Egypt; THE LAND WAS CORRUPTED BY REASON OF THE SWARM OF FLIES. (EXODUS 8:24)

36. And the Lord did that thing on the morrow, and all the cattle of Egypt died; BUT OF THE CATTLE OF THE CHILDREN OF ISRAEL DIED NOT ONE. (EXODUS 9:6)

37. And it shall become small dust in all the land of Egypt, and shall BE A BOIL BREAKING FORTH WITH BLAINS UPON MAN, and upon beast, throughout all the land of Egypt. (EXODUS 9:9)

38. Behold, tomorrow about this time I WILL CAUSE IT TO RAIN A VERY GRIEVOUS HAIL such as hath not been in Egypt since the foundation thereof even until now. (EXODUS 9:18)

39. And the Lord said unto Moses stretch out thine hand over the land of Egypt FOR THE LOCUSTS that they may come up upon the land of Egypt, and EAT EVERY HERB OF THE LAND EVEN ALL THAT THE HAIL HATH LEFT. (EXODUS 10:12)

40. And the Lord said unto Moses, stretch out thine hand TOWARD HEAVEN, THAT THERE MAY BE DARKNESS over the land of Egypt, even darkness which may be felt. (EXODUS 10:21)

41. And Moses and Aaron did all these wonders before Pharaoh: and the Lord hardened Pharaoh's heart SO THAT HE WOULD NOT LET THE CHILDREN OF ISRAEL GO OUT OF HIS LAND. (EXODUS 11:10)

42. And they shall take of the blood, and strike it on THE TWO SIDE POST AND ON THE UPPER DOOR POST OF THE HOUSE, wherein they shall eat it. (EXODUS 12:7

43. And the blood shall be to you for A TOKEN UPON THE HOUSE WHERE YE ARE: AND WHEN I SEE THE BLOOD, I WILL PASS OVER YOU and the plague shall not be upon you to destroy you, when I smite the land of Egypt. (EXODUS 12:13)`

44. And ye shall observe this thing for a ordinance to thee and to thy sons FOR EVER (EXODUS 12:24)

45. That ye shall say, IT IS THE SACRIFICE OF THE LORD'S PASSOVER, who passed over the houses of the children of Israel in Egypt, when he smote the Egyptians, and delivered our houses. AND THE PEOPLE BOWED THE HEAD AND WORSHIPPED. (EXODUS 12:27)

46. And it came to pass, that at midnight the Lord smote all the firstborn in the land of Egypt, from the FIRSTBORN OF PHARAOH that sat on his throne unto the firstborn of the captive that was in the dungeon; and ALL THE FIRSTBORN OF CATTLE. (EXODUS 12:29)

47. And Pharaoh rose up in the night, he, and all his servants, and all the Egyptians; and there was a great cry in Egypt; FOR THERE WAS NOT A HOUSE WHERE THERE WAS NOT ONE DEAD. (EXODUS 12:30)

48. And he called for Moses and Aaron by night, and said RISE UP, AND GET YOU FORTH FROM AMONG MY PEOPLE, both ye and the children of Israel; and go, SERVE THE LORD, as ye have said.(EXODUS 12:31)

49. And the children of Israel did according to the word of MOSES; and they borrowed of the Egyptians jewels of silver and jewels of gold, and raiment. And

the Lord gave the people FAVOUR IN THE SIGHT OF THE EGYPTIANS, so that they lent unto them SUCH THINGS AS THEY REQUIRED. And they spoiled the Egyptians. (EXODUS 12:35-36)

50. And it came to pass the selfsame day, that the Lord did bring the CHILDREN OF ISRAEL out of the land of Egypt by their armies. (EXODUS 12:51)

51. And the Lord spake unto Moses, saying, sanctify unto me all the FIRSTBORN, whatsoever openeth the womb among THE CHILDREN OF ISRAEL, both of man and of beast: IT IS MINE. (EXODUS 13:1-2)

52. And it shall be for a TOKEN upon thine hand, and for frontlets between thine eyes; FOR THY STRENGTH OF HAND the Lord brought us forth OUT OF EGYPT. (EXODUS 13:16)

53. And Moses took THE BONES OF JOSEPH WITH HIM: for he had straitly sworn the children of Israel saying God will surely visit you; AND YE SHALL CARRY UP MY BONES AWAY HENCE WITH YOU. (EXODUS 13:19)

54. And the Lord went before them by day IN A PILLAR OF CLOUD, to lead them the way; and by night IN A PILLAR OF FIRE, to give them light to go by day and night. (EXODUS 13:21)

55. And I will harden Pharaoh's heart, THAT HE SHALL FOLLOW AFTER THEM; and I will be honored upon Pharaoh, and upon all his host; that the Egyptians MAY KNOW that I AM the Lord. And they did so. (EXODUS 14:4)

56. And Moses said unto the people, FEAR YE NOT, STAND STILL AND SEE THE SALVATION OF THE LORD, which he will show to you today; for the Egyptians whom ye have seen today, ye shall see them again NO MORE FOR EVER. The Lord shall fight for you, AND YE SHALL HOLD YOUR PEACE. (EXODUS 14:13-14)

57. And Moses stretched out his hand over the sea; and the Lord caused the sea to go back by a strong EAST WIND all that night, and MADE THE SEA DRY LAND and the waters were divided. And THE CHILDREN OF ISRAEL went into the midst of the sea upon the DRY GROUND and the waters were a wall unto them on their RIGHT HAND AND ON THEIR LEFT. (EXODUS 14:21-22)

58. And the waters returned, and covered the chariots, and the horseman, and all the host of Pharaoh that came into the sea after them: THERE REMAINED NOT SO MUCH AS ONE OF THEM. (EXODUS 14:28)

59. Then sang Moses and the children of Israel this song unto the Lord, and spake, saying, I WILL SING UNTO THE LORD, FOR HE HATH TRIUMPHED GLORIOUSLY; THE HORSE AND HIS RIDER HATH BEEN THROWN INTO THE SEA. (EXODUS 15:1)

60. And Miriam the prophetess, THE SISTER OF AARON took a timbrel in her hand; and all the women went out after her WITH TIMBREL AND WITH DANCES. (EXODUS 15:20)

61. And the people murmured against Moses, saying, WHAT SHALL WE DRINK? And he cried unto the Lord and the LORD SHOWED HIM A TREE, which when he had cast into the waters, THE WATER WAS MADE SWEET; there he made for them a statute and an ordinance, and there he proved them. (EXODUS 15:24-25)

62. And said, if thou wilt diligently hearken to the voice of the Lord thy God AND WILT DO THAT WHICH IS RIGHT IN HIS SIGHT, and wilt give ear to his commandments and keep all his statutes, I will put none of these DISEASES UPON THEE, which I have brought upon the Egyptians; FOR I AM THE LORD THAT HEALETH THEE. (EXODUS 15:26)

63. Then said the Lord unto Moses , behold, I WILL RAIN BREAD FROM HEAVEN FOR YOU; and the people shall go out and gather a certain rate every day, THAT I MAY PROVE THEM, whether they will walk in my law or no. (EXODUS 16:4)

64. And Moses said, this shall be when the Lord shall give you in the evening flesh to eat, and in the morning bread to the full; for that the Lord heareth your murmurings which ye murmur against him; and what are we? YOUR MURMURING ARE NOT AGAINST US, BUT AGAINST THE LORD. (EXODUS 16:8)

65. Six days ye shall gather it; but on the seventh day, which is the SABBATH IN IT THERE SHALL BE NONE. (EXODUS 16:26)

66. Behold, I will stand before thee there upon the rock in Horeb; and thou shalt smite the rock, AND THERE SHALL COME WATER OUT OF IT that the people may drink. And Moses did so in the sight of the elders of Israel. (EXODUS 17:6)

67. And it came to pass on the morrow, that Moses sat to judge the people; and the people STOOD BY MOSES FROM THE MORNING UNTO THE EVENING. (EXODUS 18:13)

68. And Moses said unto his father-in-law, BECAUSE THE PEOPLE COME UNTO ME TO INQUIRE OF GOD. When they have a matter, they come unto me; AND I JUDGE BETWEEN ONE AND ANOTHER, and I do make them know the statutes of God, and his laws. (EXODUS 18:15-16)

69. And Moses chose able men out of all Israel, and make them heads over the people, rulers of thousands, rulers of hundreds, rulers of fifties and rulers of tens. And they judged the people at all seasons; THE HARD CAUSES THEY BROUGHT UNTO MOSES but every small matter they judged themselves. (EXODUS 18:25-26)

70. And Moses went up unto God, and the LORD CALLED UNTO HIM out of the mountain, saying, , thus shall thou say to the house of Jacob, and tell the children of Israel; ye have seen what I did unto the Egyptians AND HOW I BARE YOU ON EAGLES' WINGS, AND BROUGHT YOU UNTO MYSELF. Now therefore, if ye will obey my voice indeed, and keep my COVENANT, then ye shall be a PECULIAR TREASURE unto me above all people; for all the earth is mine. And ye shall be unto me a kingdom of priests, and an holy nation. THESE ARE THE WORDS WHICH THOU SHALT SPEAK UNTO THE CHILDREN OF ISRAEL. (EXODUS 19:3-6)

71. And all the people saw the THUNDERING, and the LIGHTINGS and the noise of the TRUMPET, and the mountain SMOKING; and when the people saw it, they removed, and stood afar off. (EXODUS 20:18)

72. Read/list/underline the TEN COMMANDMENTS. (EXODUS 20:2-17)

73. And the Lord said unto Moses, thus thou shalt say unto the children of Israel YE HAVE SEEN THAT I HAVE TALKED WITH YOU FROM HEAVEN. (EXODUS 20:22)

74. And he that smiteth his father or his mother, SHALL BE SURELY PUT TO DEATH. (EXODUS 21:15)

75. If the theft be certainly found in his hand alive, whether it be ox or ass or sheep HE SHALL RESTORE DOUBLE. (EXODUS 22:4)

76. But if thou shalt indeed OBEY HIS VOICE, AND DO ALL THAT I SPEAK; then I will be an enemy unto thine enemies and an adversary unto thine adversaries. (EXDOUS 23:22)

77. And he said unto Moses, come up unto the Lord, THOU AND AARON, NADAB, AND ABIHU AND seventy of the elders of Israel, and worship ye afar off. (EXODUS 24:1)

78. And Moses came and told the people all the words of the Lord, and all the judgments; and all the people answered with one voice, and said ALL THE WORDS WHICH THE LORD HATH SAID WILL WE DO. And Moses wrote all the words of the Lord, and rose up early in the morning, and built an altar under the hill, and TWELVE PILLARS, to THE TWELVE TRIBES OF ISRAEL. (EXODUS 24:3-4)

79. And Moses took the blood, and SPRINKLED IT ON THE PEOPLE, AND SAID, BEHOLD, THE BLOOD OF THE COVENANT, which the Lord hath made with you concerning all these words. (EXODUS 24:8)

80. And Moses went into the midst of the cloud, and got him up into the mount AND MOSES WAS IN THE MOUNT FORTY DAYS AND FORTY NIGHTS. (EXODUS 24:18)

81. Speak unto the children of Israel, that they BRING ME AN OFFERING; of every man that giveth it willingly with his heart ye shall take my offering (EXODUS 25:2)

82. Oil for light, SPICES FOR ANOINTING OIL and for sweet incense. (EXODUS 25:2)

83. Thou shalt also make a TABLE OF SHILLIN WOOD ; two cubits shall be the length thereof, and a cubit the breadth thereof AND A CUBIT AND A HALF THE HEIGHT THEREOF. (EXODUS 25:23)

84. Moreover thou shalt make the tabernacle with ten curtains of fine twined linen, and blue, and purple, and scarlet; WITH CHERUBIMS OF CUNNING WORK SHALT THOU MAKE THEM. (EXODUS 26:1)

85. And thou shall make a covering for the tent OF RAMS SKIN DYED RED and a covering above OF BADGERS SKINS. (EXODUS 26:14)

86. And thou shalt make AN ALTAR of shittim wood, five cubits long, and five cubits broad; and the altar shall be foursquare: and the height thereof SHALL BE THREE CUBITS. (EXODUS 27:1)

87. Hollow with boards shalt thou make it: AS IT WAS SHOWN THEE IN THE MOUNT, so shall they make it. (EXODUS 27:8)

88. And thou shall make holy garments FOR AARON THY BROTHER FOR GLORY AND FOR BEAUTY. (EXODUS 28:2)

89. And thou shalt take two onyx stones, and grave on them THE NAMES OF THE CHILDREN OF ISRAEL: six of their names on one stone and other six names of the rest on the stone, ACCORDING TO THEIR BIRTH. (EXODUS 28:9-10)

90. And thou shall put them upon Aaron thy brother, and his sons with him; AND SHALT ANOINT THEM, AND CONSECRATE THEM, AND SANCTIFY THEM that they may minister unto me in the PRIEST'S OFFICE. (EXODUS 28:41)

91. Then shall thou take the ANOINTING OIL, AND POUR IT UPON HIS HEAD, and anoint him. (EXODUS 29:7)

92. And they shall eat those things wherewith THE ATONEMENT WAS MADE, TO CONSECRATE AND TO SANCTIFY THEM; but a stranger shall not eat thereof, because they are holy. (EXODUS 29:33)

93. And they shall know that I AM THE LORD THEIR GOD, that brought them forth out of the land of Egypt, that I may dwell among them; I AM THE LORD THEIR GOD. (EXODUS 29:46)

94. And the rich shall not give more, AND THE POOR SHALL NOT GIVE LESS THAN HALF A SHEKEL, when they give an offering unto the Lord to make an ATONEMENT for your souls. (EXODUS 30:15)

95. I have filled him WITH THE SPIRIT OF GOD, in wisdom, and in understanding, and in knowledge, and in all manner of workmanship. (EXODUS 31:3)

96. Speak thou also unto the children of Israel, saying, verily Sabbath ye shall keep FOR IT IS A SIGN BETWEEN ME AND YOU throughout your generation that ye may know that I am the Lord that doth sanctify you. (EXODUS 31:13)

97. And all the people brake off the golden earrings which were in their ears, AND BROUGHT THEM UNTO AARON. (EXODUS 32:3)

98. And the Lord said unto Moses GO, GET THEE DOWN, for thy people, which thou broughtest out of the land of Egypt, HAVE CORRUPTED THEMSELVES. (EXODUS 32:7)

99. And the Lord said unto Moses, I have seen this people, and, behold, IT IS A STIFFNECKED PEOPLE. (EXODUS 32:9)

100. And the Lord REPENTED of the evil which he thought to DO UNTO HIS PEOPLE. (EXODUS 32:14)

101. And it came to pass, as soon as he came nigh unto the camp, that HE SAW THE CALF, AND THE DANCING, and Moses anger waxed hot, and he cast the tables out of his hands, and BRAKE THEN BENEATH THE MOUNT. (EXODUS 32:19)

102. Then Moses stood in the gate of the camp, and said, WHO IS ON THE LORD'S SIDE? Let him come unto me. And ALL THE SONS OF LEVI gathered themselves together unto him. (EXODUS 32:26)

103. And the Lord said unto Moses, whosoever hath sinned against me, HIM WILL I BLOT OUT OF MY BOOK. (EXODUS 32:33)

104. And Moses took THE TABERNACLES and pitched it without the camp, afar off from the camp, and called it THE TABERNACLES OF THE CONGREGATION. And it came to pass, that every one which sought the Lord

went out unto the tabernacle of the congregation, which was without the camp. (EXODUS 33:7)

105. And the Lord said unto Moses, I will do this thing also that thou hast spoken: FOR THOU HAST FOUND GRACE IN MY SIGHT, AND I KNOW THEE BY NAME. (EXODUS 33:17)

106. And the Lord said unto Moses, hew thee two tables of stone like unto the first; and I will write upon these tables the words that were in the first tables, WHICH THOU BRAKEST. (EXODUS 34:1)

107. For thou shall worship no other god: for the Lord, whose name is jealous, IS A JEALOUS GOD. (EXODUS 34:14)

108. But the FIRSTLING of an ass thou shall redeem with a lamb; and IF THOU REDEEM HIM NOT, then shalt thou break his neck. All the FIRSTBORN of any sons thou shall redeem. AND NONE SHALL APPEAR BEFORE ME EMPTY. (EXODUS 34:20)

109. And the Lord said unto Moses, write thou these words; for after the tenor of these words I HAVE MADE A COVENANT WITH THEE AND WITH ISRAEL. And he was there with the Lord FORTY DAYS AND FORTY NIGHTS; he did neither eat bread, nor drink water. And he wrote UPON THE TABLES THE WORD OF THE COVENENT, THE TEN COMMANDMENTS. And it came to pass, when Moses came down from MOUNT SINAI with the two tables of testimony in Moses' hand, when he came down from the mount, that Moses wist not that THE SKIN OF HIS FACE SHONE WHILE HE TALKED WITH HIM. And when Aaron and all the children of Israel saw Moses, behold, THE SKIN OF HIS FACE SHONE. And they were afraid to come nigh him. (EXODUS 34:27-30)

110. And till Moses had done speaking with them, HE PUT A VEIL ON HIS FACE. (EXODUS 34:33)

111. And Moses gathered all the congregation of the children of Israel together, and said unto them, these are words which the Lord hath COMMANDED THAT YE SHOULD DO THEM. (EXODUS 35:1)

112. And Moses said unto the children of Israel, see, the Lord hath called by name BEZABEEL THE SON OF URI, THE SON OF HUR, OF THE TRIBE OF

JUDAH, and he hath filled HIM WITH THE SPIRIT OF GOD, in wisdom, in understanding, and in knowledge, and in all mammer of workmanship. (EXODUS 35:30-31)

113. And he hath put IN HIS HEART THAT HE MAY TEACH, both he and Aholiab, the son of Ahisamach, of THE TRIBE OF DAN. (EXODUS 35:34)

114. And they spake unto Moses saying, THE PEOPLE BRING MUCH MORE THAN ENOUGH for the service of the work, which the Lord commanded to make. (EXODUS 36:5)

115. And the five pillars of it with their hooks; and he overlaid their chapters and their fillets with gold: BUT THEIR FIVE SOCKETS WERE OF BRASS. (EXODUS 36:38)

116. And he made his seven lamps, and his snuffers, and his snuffdishes OF PURE GOLD. (EXODUS 37:23)

117. And he made THE HOLY ANOINTING OIL and the pure incense of sweet spices, according to the work of the apothecary. (EXODUS 37:29)

118. This is the sum of the tabernacle even of the tabernacle of testimony as it was counted, according to the commandment of Moses, FOR THE SERVICE OF THE LEVITES by the hand of ITHAMAR SON OF AARON THE PREIST. (EXODUS 38:21)

119. And Bezaleet the son of URI, the son of HUR, OF THE TRIBE OF JUDAH, made all that the Lord commanded Moses. (EXODUS 38:22)

120. And of the blue, and purple, and scarlet, they made cloth of service, to do service in the holy place, AND MAKE THE HOLY GARMENTS FOR AARON, as the Lord commanded MOSES. (EXODUS 39:1)

121. Thus was all the work of the tabernacle of the tent of the congregation finished: and the children of Israel did according to all that the Lord commanded MOSED, SO DID THEY. (EXODUS 39:32)

122. And Moses did look upon all the work, AND BEHOLD, THEY HAD DONE IT AS THE LORE HAD COMMANDED, even so had they done it; AND MOSES BLESSED THEM. (EXODUS 39:43).

123. And Moses and Aaron and his sons WASHED THEIR HANDS AND THEIR FEET THEREAT; when they WENT INTO the tent of the congregation, and when they CAME NEAR unto the altar, THEY WASHED as the Lord commanded Moses. And he reared up the court round about the tabernacle and the altar and set up the HANGING OF THE COURT GATE. So Moses finished the work. Then a cloud covered the tent of the congregation AND THE GLORY OF THE LORD FILLED THE TABERNACLE. (EXODUS 40:31-34)

124. For the cloud of the Lord was upon the tabernacle BY DAY AND FIRE WAS ON IT BY NIGHT, in the sight of all the house of Israel, throughout all their journeys. (EXODUS 40:38)

The End EXODUS

LEVITICUS

1. If his offering be a burnt sacrifice of the herd, LET HIM OFFER A MALE WITHOUT BLEMISH; he shall offer it of his own voluntary will at the door of the tabernacle of the congregation BEFORE THE LORD. And he shall put his hand upon the head of the burnt offering; and it shall be ACCEPTED FOR HIM TO MAKE ATONEMENT FOR HIM. ((LEVITICUS 1:3-4)

2. And when any will offer meat offering unto the Lord, his offering SHALL BE OF FINE FLOUR; AND HE SHALL POUR OIL UPON IT, and put frankincense thereon. (LEVITICUS 2:1)

3. As for the oblation of the FIRSTFRUIT, YE SHALL OFFER THEM UNTO THE LORD: but they shall not be burnt on the altar for a sweet savour. (LEVITICUS 2:12)

4. And if his oblation be a sacrifice of PEACE OFFERING, if he offer it of the herd; whether it be a male or female, he shall offer it WITHOUT BLEMISH BEFORE THE LORD. (LEVITICUS 3:1)

5. If the priest that is anointed do sin ACCORDING TO THE SIN OF THE PEOPLE; then let him bring for his sin, which he hath sinned, a young bullock without blemish unto the Lord FOR A SIN OFFERING. (LEVITICUS 4:3)

6. And if a soul sin, and commit any of these things which are forbidden to be done by the commandments of the Lord though he wist it not, yet is he guilty, AND SHALL BEAR HIS INIQUITY. (LEVITICUS 5:17)

7. And the priest shall make an ATONEMENT FOR HIM before the Lord: and it shall be forgiven him for any thing of all that he hath done IN TRESPASSING THEREIN. (LEVITICUS 6:7)

8. And the priest shall burn the fat upon the altar: but the breast shall be AARON'S AND HIS SONS. (LEVITICUS 7:31)

9. And Moses took the anointing oil, AND ANOINTED THE TABERNACLE and all that was therein, AND SANCTIFIED THEM . (LEVITICUS 8:10)

10. And he poured of the anointing oil upon AARON'S HEAD, AND ANOINTED HIM to sanctify him. (LEVITICUS 8:12)

11. Aaron therefore went unto the altar, and slew the calf of the sin offering, WHICH WAS FOR HIMSELF. (LEVITICUS 9:8)

12. And Aaron lifted up his hand TOWARD THE PEOPLE AND BLESSED THEM, and came down from offering of the SIN offering, and the BURNT offering, and PEACE OFFERINGS. (LEVITICUS 9:22)

13. And Nadab and Abihu, the SONS OF AARON, took either of his censer, and put fire therein, and put incense thereon, and offered STRANGE FIRE before the Lord, WHICH HE COMMANDED THEM NOT. And there went out fire from the Lord and DEVOURED THEM, AND THEY DIE BEFORE THE LORD. (LEVITICUS 10:1-2)

14. And Moses spake unto Aaron, and unto Eleazar and unto Ithamar, HIS SONS THAT WER LEFT, take the meat offering that remained of the offering of the Lord made by fire, and eat it without leaven beside the altar : FOR IT IS MOST HOLY. (LEVITICUS 10:12)

15. These shall ye eat of all that are in the waters: whatsoever hath FINS AND SCALES in the waters, in the sea, and in the rivers, THEM SHALL YE EAT. (LEVITICUS 11:9)

16. For I AM the Lord that bringeth you up out of the land of Egypt, to be your God: ye shall therefore be holy, FOR I AM HOLY. (LEVITICUS 11:45)

17. Speak unto the children of Israel, saying, IF A WOMAN HAVE CONCEIVED SEED, AND BORN A MAN CHILD: THEN she shall be unclean seven days; according to the days of the separation for her infirmity shall she be unclean. And in the eighth day THE FLESH OF HIS FORESKIN SHALL BE CIRCUMCISED. (LEVITICUS 12:2-3)

18. And the priest shall look on the plague in the skin of the flesh: AND WHEN THE HAIR IN THE PLAGUE IS TURNED WHITE, and the plague in sight be deeper than the skin of his flesh, IT IS A PLAGUE OF LEPROSY; and the priest shall look on him, and pronounce him UNCLEAN. (LEVITICUS 13:3)

19. Then the priest shall consider: and , behold, IF THE LEPROSY HAVE COVERED ALL HIS FLESH he shall pronounce him clean that hath the plague; it is all turned white: HE IS CLEAN. (LEVITICUS 13:13)

20. This is the law of the plague of leprosy in a garment of woollen or linen, either in the warp, or woof, or any thing of skin, TO PRONOUNCE IT CLEAN OR TO PRONOUNCE IT UNCLEAN. (LEVITICUS 13:59)

21. And he that is to be cleansed shall wash his clothes, and shave off all his hair, and wash himself in water, that he may be clean: and after that he shall COME INTO THE CAMP and shall tarry abroad out of his tent SEVEN DAYS. (LEVITICUS 14:8)

22. And the Lord spake unto MOSES and unto AARON, saying, when ye be come into THE LAND OF CANAAN which I give to you for a possession, and I put the PLAGUE OF LEPROSY in a house of the land of your possession: and he that owneth the house shall COME AND TELL THE PRIEST, saying, it seemeth to me there is as it were A PLAGUE IN THE HOUSE. (LEVITICUS 14:34-35)

23. To teach when it is UNCLEAN, and when it is CLEAN; this is the law of leprosy. (LEVITICUS 14:57)

24. And the vessel of earth, that he toucheth which hath the issue, shall be broken: AND EVERY VESSEL OF WOOD SHALL BE RINSED IN WATER. (LEVITICUS 15:12)

25. And the priest shall offer them, the one for a sin offering, and the other for a burnt offering, and the priest shall make AN ATONEMENT for him before the Lord for his issue. (LEVITICUS 15:15)

26. But if she be cleansed of her issue, then she shall NUMBER TO HERSELF SEVEN DAYS. (LEVITICUS 15:28)

27. And he shall make an atonement for the holy place, because of the UNCLEANNESS OF THE CHILDREN OF ISRAEL, and because of their TRANSGRESSIONS IN ALL THEIR SINS; and so shall he do for the tabernacle of the congregation, that remained among them in the midst of their uncleanness. (LEVITICUS 16:16)

28. For on that day shall the priest MAKE AN ATONEMENT FOR YOU, to cleanse you, that ye may be clean FROM ALL YOUR SINS before the Lord. It shall be a SABBATH OF REST UNTO YOU, and ye shall afflict your souls, by a statue for ever. (LEVITICUS 16:30-31)

29. And this shall be an EVERLASTING STATUE UNTO YOU, to make an atonement for the CHILDREN OF ISRAEL for all their sins ONCE A YEAR. And he did as the Lord commanded Moses. (LEVITICUS 16:34)

30. And the priest shall sprinkle the blood UNPON THE ALTAR OF THE LORD at the door of the TABERNACLE OF THE CONGREGATION, and burn the fat for a sweet savour unto the Lord. (LEVITICUS 17:6)

31. But if he wash them not, nor bathe his flesh: THEN HE SHALL BEAR HIS INIQUITY. (LEVITICUS 17:16)

32. Ye shall therefore keep my statutes, and my judgments: WHICH IF A MAN DO, he shall live in them: I AM the Lord. (LEVITICUS 18:5)

33. None of you shall approach to any THAT IS NEAR OF KIN TO HIM to uncover their nakedness: I AM the Lord. (LEVITICUS 18:6)

34. Moreover thou shall not lie carnally with thy neighbor's wife, TO DEFILE THYSELF WITH HER. (LEVITICUS 18:20)

35. And the Lord spake unto Moses, saying, speak unto all THE CONGREGATION of the children of Israel, and say unto them ye shall be HOLY; for I the Lord your God AM HOLY. (LEVITICUS 9:1-2)

36. And if ye offer a sacrifice of peace offering unto the Lord, ye shall offer it AT YOUR OWN WILL. (LEVITICUS 19:5)

37. Ye shall not steal, neither deal falsely, NEITHER LIE ONE TO ANOTHER. (LEVITICUS 19:11)

38. If a man also lie with mankind, AS HE LIETH WITH A WOMAN, both of them have committed an abomination; they shall surely be put to death; their blood shall be upon them. (LEVITICUS 20:13)

39. And ye shall be HOLY unto me: for I the Lord am holy, and have severed you from other people, THAT YE SHOULD BE MINE. (LEVITICUS 20:26)

40. But he shall not defile himself, BEING A CHIEF MAN AMONG HIS PEOPLE, to profane himself. (LEVITICUS 21:4)

41. And Moses told it unto Aaron, and to his sons, and UNTO ALL THE CHILDREN OF ISRAEL. (LEVITICUS 21:24)

42. That which dieth of itself, or is torn with beasts, HE SHALL NOT EAT TO DEFILE HIMSELF THEREWITH; I AM the Lord. (LEVITICUS 22:8)

43. That brought you out of THE LAND OF EGYPT, to be your God: I AM the Lord. (LEVITICUS 22:33)

44. Speak unto the children of Israel, and say unto them, concerning THE FEAST OF THE LORD which ye shall proclaim to be HOLY CONVOCATION, even these are my feasts. (LEVITICUS 23:2)

45. And the Lord spake unto Moses, saying, speak unto the children of Israel, and say unto them, WHEN YE BE COME INTO THE LAND WHICH I GIVE UNTO YOU, and shall reap the harvest thereof, then ye shall bring a SHEAF OF THE FIRSTFRUIT OF YOUR HARVEST UNTO THE PRIEST. (LEVITICUS 23:9-10)

46. And ye shall do no work in that same day; FOR IT IS A DAY OF ATONEMENT, to make an atonement for you before the LORD YOUR GOD. (LEVITICUS 23:28)

47. And Moses declared unto THE CHILDREN OF ISRAEL, the feast of the Lord. (LEVITICUS 23:44)

48. Command the children of Israel, that they bring unto thee PURE OIL OLIVE BEATEN for the light, to cause the lamps to burn CONTINUALLY. (LEVITICUS 24:2)

49. Speak unto the children of Israel, and say unto them, when ye come into the land which I give you, then shall the land KEEP A SABBATH UNTO THE LORD. Six years thou shalt sow thy field, and SIX YEARS thou shalt prune thy vineyard, and gather in the fruit thereof; but in the SEVENETH YEARS shall be a SABBATH OF REST unto the land, a SABBATH for the Lord; thou shalt neither sow thy field, nor prune thy vineyard. (LEVITICUS 25:2-4)

50. Then shall thou cause the trumpet of the jubilee to sound on THE TENTH DAY OF THE SEVENTH MONTH, in the day of atonement shall ye make the trumpet sound throughout all your land. (LEVITICUS 25:9)

51. Then I will command my BLESSING UPON YOU IN THE SIXTH YEAR , and it shall bring forth fruit for three years. (LEVITICUS 25:21)

52. For unto me the children of Israel are servants; THEY ARE MY SERVANTS whom I brought forth out of the land of Egypt: I AM the Lord your God. (LEVITICUS 25:55)

53. Ye shall keep my Sabbath AND REVERENCE MY SANCTUARY: I AM the Lord. (LEVITICUS 26:2)

54. If ye walk in my statutes, and keep my commandments, AND DO THEM; then I will give you rain in DUE SEASON, and the land shall yield her INCREASE and the trees of the field shall yield their fruit. (LEVITICUS 26:2-4)

55. And five of you shall CHASE AN HUNDRED and an hundred of you shall put TEN THOUSANDS TO FLIGHT; and your enemies shall fall before you by the sword. For I will have RESPECT UNTO YOU, and make you fruitful and multiply you, AND ESTABLISH MY COVENANT WITH YOU. (LEVITICUS 26:8-9)

56. I AM the Lord your God, which brought you forth out of the land of Egypt, that ye should not be their bondmen; and I HAVE BROKEN THE BANDS OF YOUR YOKE, and made you go upright. (LEVITICUS 26:13)

57. Then will I also walk contrary unto you , and will punish you yet SEVEN TIMES FOR YOUR SINS. (LEVITICUS 26:24)

58. If they shall confess their iniquity, and the iniquity of their fathers , with their trespass which they trespassed against me, and that also THEY HAVE WALKED CONTRARY UNTO ME; and that I also have walked contrary unto them, and have brought them into the land of their enemies; IF THEN THEIR UNCIRCUMCISED HEARTS BE HUMBLED, and they then accept of the punishment of their iniquity. Then will I REMEMBER MY COVENANT WITH JACOB, AND ALSO MY COVENANT WITH ISAAC AND ALSO MY COVENANT WITH ABRAHAM WILL I REMEMBER and I will remember the land. (LEVITICUS 26:40-42

59. And the Lord spake unto Moses, saying, speak unto the children of Israel, and say unto them, WHEN A MAN SHALL MAKE A SINGULAR VOW, the persons shall be for the Lord by thy estimation. (LEVITICUS 27:1-2)

60. Only the firstling of the beasts, WHICH SHOULD BE THE LORD'S FIRSTLING, no man shall sanctify it; whether it be ox, or sheep; IT IS THE LORD'S. (LEVITICUS 27:26)

61. And all the tithe of the land, whether of the seed of the land, or of the fruit of the tree, IS THE LORD'S: IT IS HOLY UNTO THE LORD. (LEVITICUS 27:30)

62. And concerning the tithe of the herd, or of the flock, even of whatsoever passeth under the rod, THE TENTH SHALL BE HOLY UNTO THE LORD. (LEVITICUS 27:32)

63. These are the commandments , which the Lord commanded MOSES for the children of Israel in Mount Sinai. (LEVITICUS 27:34)

The End LEVITICUS

NUMBERS

1. And the Lord spake unto Moses IN THE WILDERNESS OF SINAI in the tabernacle of the congregation, on the first day of the second month, IN THE SECOND YEAR after they were come out of the land of Egypt, saying, take ye the sum of all the congregation of the children of Israel, after their families, by the house of their fathers, WITH THE NUMBER OF THEIR NAMES, every male by their polls: from twenty years old and upward, all that are able to go forth to war in Israel. THOU AND AARON SHALL NUMBER THEM BY THEIR ARMIES. And with you there shall be a man OF EVERY TRIBE; every one head of the house of his fathers. (NUMBERS 1:1-4)

2. Even all they were numbered were SIX HUNDRED THOUSAND AND THREE THOUSAND AND FIVE HUNDRED AND FIFTY. But the Levites after the tribe of their fathers were not numbered among them. (NUMBERS 1:46-47)

3. But thou shall APPOINT THE LEVITES OVER THE TABERNACLE OF TESTIMONY, and over all the vessels thereof, and over all things that belong to it; they shall bear the tabernacle, and all vessels thereof; and they shall minister unto it, and shall encamp round about the tabernacle. (NUMBERS 1:50)

4. Every man of the children of Israel shall PITCH BY HIS OWN STANDARD, with the ensign of their father's house; for off about the tabernacle of the congregation SHALL THEY PITCH. (NUMBERS 2:2)

5. Then the tribe of Benjamin and the captain of the sons of Benjamin shall be ABIDAN THE SON OF GIDEON. (NUMBERS 2:22)

6. And Nadab and Abihu DIED BEFORE THE LORD, WHEN THEY OFFERED STRANGE FIRE, before the Lord, in the wilderness of Sinai, and they had not children; and Eleazar and Ithamar ministered in the priest's office in the sight of AARON THEIR FATHER. (NUMBERS 3:4)

7. And they shall keep his charge, AND THE CHARGE of the whole congregation before the tabernacle of the congregation, to do THE SERVICE OF THE TABERNACLE (NUMBERS 3:7)

8. In the number of all the males, from a month old and upward were eight thousand and six hundred, KEEPING THE CHARGE OF THE SANCTUARY. (NUMBERS 3:28)

9. And Moses numbered, as the Lord commanded him, ALL THE FIRSTBORN AMONG the children of Israel. (NUMBERS 3:42)

10. And Moses took THE REDEMPTION MONEY of them that were over and above them that were redeemed by the LEVITES. (NUMBERS 3:49)

11. This shall be the service of the SONS OF KOHATH in the tabernacle of the congregation, about THE MOST HOLY THINGS. (NUMBERS 4:4)

12. And Moses and Aaron and the CHIEF OF THE CONGREGATION numbered the sons of the Kohathites after their families, and after the house of their fathers (NUMBERS 4:34)

13. According to the commandment of the Lord THEY WERE NUMBERED BY THE HAND OF MOSES, every one according to his service, and according to his burden; thus were they numbered of him AS THE LORD COMMANDED MOSES. (NUMBERS 4:49)

14. Command the children of Israel, that they put out of the camp EVERY LEPER, AND EVERY ONE THAT HATH AN ISSUE, and whosoever is defiled by the dead. (NUMBERS 5:2)

15. And the priest shall write these curses in a book, AND HE SHALL BLOT THEM OUT with the bitter water. (NUMBERS 5:23)

16. Then shall the man be guiltless from iniquity, and this woman SHALL BEAR HER INIQUITY. (NUMBERS 5:31)

17. Speak unto the children of Israel, and say unto them, when either man or woman shall separate themselves TO VOW A VOW OF A NAZARITE, to separate themselves unto the Lord: He shall separate himself from WINE AND STRONG DRINKS and shall drink no vinegar of wine, or vinegar of strong drink, neither shall he drink any liquor of grapes, NOR EAT MOIST GRAPES OR DRIED. (NUMBERS 6:2-3)

18. All the days of the vow of his separation there SHALL NO RAZOR COME UPON HIS HEAD; until the days be fulfilled, in the which he separateth himself unto the Lord, he shall be holy, and shall let the locks of the hair OF HIS HEAD GROW. (NUMBERS 6:5)

19. All the days that he separateth himself unto the Lord, he shall come at NO DEAD BODY. (NUMBERS 6:6)

20. All the days of his separation he is HOLY UNTO THE LORD. (NUMBERS 6:8)

21. And this is the law of the Nazarite WHEN THE DAYS OF HIS SEPARATION ARE FULFILLED; he shall be brought unto the door of the TABERNACLE OF THE CONGREGATION. (NUMBERS 6:13)

22. But unto the sons of Kohath HE GAVE NONE; because the service of the sanctuary belonging unto them was that they should BEAR UPON THEIR SHOULDERS. (NUMBERS 7:9)

23. On the fourth day Elizur the son of Shedeur, PRINCE OF THE CHILDRED OF REUBEN, DID OFFER: (NUMBERS 7:30)

24. On the nineth day Abidan the son of Gideon, PRINCE OF THE CHILDREN OF BENJAMIN, OFFERED: (NUMBERS 7:60)

25. On the twelfth day Ahira the son of Eran, Prince of the children of NAPHTALI, OFFERED: (NUMBERS 7:78)

26. Speak unto Aaron, and say unto him, when thou lightest the lamps THE SEVEN LAMPS SHALL GIVE LIGHT OVER AGAINST the candlestick. (NUMBERS 8:2)

27. And the Levites were purified, and they washed their clothes; and Aaron offered them as an offering before the Lord; AND AARON MADE AN ATONEMENT FOR THEM TO CLEANSE THEM. (NUMBERS 8:21)

28. And from the age of FIFTY YEARS they shall cease waiting upon the service thereof AND SHALL SERVE NO MORE. (NUMBERS 8:25)

29. Let the children of Israel also keep THE PASSOVER AT HIS APPOINTED SEASON. (NUMBERS 9:2)

30. And Moses said unto them, STAND STILL, and I will hear what the Lord will command CONCERNING YOU. (NUMBERS 9:8)

31. So it was always ; the cloud covered it by day, and the appearance OF FIRE BY NIGHT. (NUMBERS 9:16)

32. And when they shall blow with them, ALL THE ASSEMBLY SHALL ASSEMBLE THEMSELVES TO THEE at the door of the tabernacle of the congregation. (NUMBERS 10:3)

33. And the children of Israel took their journeys out of THE WILDERNESS OF SINAI and the cloud rested in the wilderness of Paran. (NUMBERS 10:12)

34. And the tabernacle was taken down and the sons of Gershon and the sons of Merari set forward, BEARING THE TABERNACLE. (NUMBERS 10:17)

35. And it came to pass when the art set forward that Moses said, rise up, Lord, and let thine enemies be scattered; AND LET THEM THAT HATE THEE FLEE BEFORE THEE. (NUMBERS 10:35)

36. And when the people COMPLAINED, it displeased the Lord; and the Lord heard it, AND HIS ANGER WAS KINDLED; and the fire of the Lord burnt among them, AND CONSUMED THEM THAT WERE in the uttermost parts of the camp. (NUMBERS 11:1)

37. I am not able to bear all this people alone, BECAUSE IT TS TOO HEAVY FOR ME. (NUMBERS 11:14)

38. And the Lord said unto Moses, gather unto me SEVENTY MEN OF THE ELDERS OF ISRAEL, whom thou knowest to be the elders of the people, and officers over them; and bring them unto the tabernacle of the congregation that they may stand there with thee. (NUMBERS 11:16)

39. And Joshua the son of Nun, the servant of Moses , one of his young men, answered and said, MY LORD MOSES, FORBID THEM. ((NUMBERS 11:28)

40. And while the flesh was YET BETWEEN THEIR TEETH, ere it was chewed, the wrath of the Lord was kindled against the people, and the Lord smote the people with a very great plague. And he called the name of that place

Kibroth-hattaavah; because there they BURIED THE PEOPLE THAT LUSTED. (NUMBERS 11:33-34)

41. And Miriam and Aaron spake against Moses BECAUSE OF THE ETHIOPIAN WOMAN WHOM HE HAD MARRIED; for he had married an Ethiopian woman. (NUMBERS 12:1)

42. And the Lord came down in the pillar of the cloud, and stood in the door of the tabernacle, AND CALLED AARON AND MIRIAM; and they both came forth. (NUMBERS 12:5)

43. And the anger of the Lord MIRIAM BECAME LEPROUS, WHITE AS SNOW, and he departed. (NUMBERS 12:9)

44. And the cloud departed from off the tabernacle; and behold, SEVEN DAYS; and Aaron looked upon Miriam, and, behold, SHE WAS LEPROUS. (NUMBERS 12:10)

45. And Miriam was shut out from the camp SEVEN DAYS; and the people journeyed not until MIRIAM WAS BROUGHT IN AGAIN. (NUMBERS 12:15)

46. And Moses by the commandment of the Lord sent them from the wilderness of Paran; ALL THOSE MEN WERE HEADS OF THE CHILDREN OF ISRAEL. (NUMBERS 13:3)

47. And Moses sent them to spy out THE LAND OF CANAAN, and said unto them, get you up this way southward, and go up into the mountain. (NUMBERS 13:17)

48. And they returned from searching of the land AFTER FORTY DAYSS. (NUMBERS 13:25)

49. And they told him, and said, we came unto the land whither thou sentest us, and SURELY IT FLOWETH WITH MILK AND HONEY; and this is the fruit of it. (NUMBERS 13:27)

50. And they brought up an evil report of the land which they had searched unto the children of Israel, saying, the land through which we have go to search it, IS A LAND THAT EATETH UP THE INHABITANTS THEREOF; and all

the people that we saw in it ARE MEN OF GREAT STATURE and we saw the GIANTS; and Anak, which come of the giants; and we were in our own sight AS GRASSHOPPERS and we were in their sight. (NUMBERS 13:32-33)

51. I the Lord have said, I will surely do it unto all this evil congregation, THAT ARE GATHERED TOGETHER AGAINS ME; in this wilderness they shall be consumed, and there they shall die. And the men, which Moses sent to search the land, who returned, AND MADE ALL THE CONGREGATION TO MURMUR AGAINST ME, by bring up a slander upon the land. Even those men that did bring up the EVIL REPORT UPON THE LAND, DIED BY THE PLAGUE before the Lord. But JOSHUA the son of Nun, and CALEB the son of Jephunneh, which were of the men that went to search the land, LIVED STILL. (NUMBERS 14:35-38)

52. According to the number that ye shall prepare, so shall ye do to EVERY ONE ACCORDING TO THEIR NUMBER. (NUMBERS 15;12)

53. One law and one manner shall be for you and for the STRANGER THAT SOJOURNED WITH YOU. (NUMBERS 15:16)

54. And the priest shall make an atonement for the SOUL THAT SINNETH IGNORANTLY, when he sinneth by ignorance before the Lord, to make an atonement for him; AND IT SHALL BE FORGIVEN HIM. (NUMBERS 15:28)

55. And they that found him gathering sticks brought him unto MOSES AND AARON, AND UNTO ALL THE CONGREGATION. (NUMBERS 15:33)

56. That ye may remember, and do all my commandments, AND BE HOLY UNTO YOUR GOD. (NUMBERS 15:40)

57. And Korah gathered all the congregation against them unto the door of the tabernacle of the congregation; AND THE GLORY OF THE LORD APPEARED UNTO ALL THE CONGREGATION. And the Lord spake unto Moses and unto Aaron, saying, separate yourselves from among this congregation, THAT I MAY CONSUME THEM IN A MOMENT. (NUMBERS 16:19-20)

58. And the earth opened her mouth, and SWALLOWED THEM UP, and their houses, and all the men that appertained unto Korah, and all their goods. (NUMBERS 16:32)

59. And thou shalt write AARON'S NAME UPON THE ROD OF LEVI; for ONE ROD shall be for the head of the house of their fathers. (NUMBERS 17:3)

60. And it shall come to pass, that the man's rod, whom I shall choose, SHALL BLOSSOM; and I will make to cease from me the murmurings of the children of Israel, whereby they murmur against you. (NUMBERS 17:5)

61. And Moses laid up the RODS before the Lord in the tabernacle of witness. And it came to pass, that on the morrow Moses went into the tabernacle of witness; and , behold, THE ROD OF AARON FOR THE HOUSE OF LEVI WAS BUDDED, and brought forth buds, and bloomed blossoms, and YIELDED ALMONDS. (NUMBERS 17:7-8)

62. And the Lord said unto Moses, bring Aaron's rod again before the testimony, TO BE KEPT AS A TOKEN AGAINST THE REBELS, and thou shall quite take away their murmurings from me, that they die not. (NUMBERS 17:10)

63. And I, behold, I have taken your brethren the Levites from among the children of Israel: to you they are given as a gift for the Lord, TO DO THE SERVICE OF THE TABERNACLE OF THE CONGREGATION. (NUMBERS18:6)

64. All the best of the oil, and all the best of the wine, and of the wheat, THE FIRSTFRUIT OF THEM WHICH THEY SHALL OFFER UNTO THE LORD, them have I given thee. (NUMBERS 18:12)

65. And, behold, I have given the children of Levi all the tenth in Israel for an inheritance, FOR THEIR SERVICE WHICH THEY SERVICE, even the service of the tabernacle of the congregation. (NUMBERS 18:21)

66. Thus speak unto the Levites, and say unto them, when ye take of the children of Israel THE TITHES which I have given you FROM THEM FOR YOUR INHERITANCE, then ye shall offer up an heave offering of it for the Lord, EVEN A TENTH PART OF THE TITHE. (NUMBERS 18:26)

67. And Eleazar the priest shall take of her blood with his finger, and sprinkle of her blood directly before the tabernacle of the congregation SEVEN TIMES. (NUMBERS 19:4)

68. And a man that is clean shall gather up the ashes of the heifer, and lay them up without the camp in a CLEAN PLACE, and it shall be kept for the congregation

of the children of Israel for a water of separation: IT IS A PURIFICATION FOR SIN. (NUMBERS 19:9)

69. Then came the children of Israel, even the whole congregation, into the desert of Zin in the first month: and the people abode in Kadesh; and MIRIAM DIED THERE, AND WAS BURIED THERE. (NUMBERS 20:1)

70. And Moses lifted up his hand, and with his rod he SMOTE THE ROCK TWICE and the water came out abundantly and the congregation drank and their beasts also. (NUMBERS 20:11)

71. And the Lord spake unto Moses and Aaron, because ye believed me not, to sanctify me in the eyes of the children of Israel, THEREFORE YE SHALL NOT bring this congregation into the land which I have given them. (NUMBERS 20:12)

72. Aaron shall be gathered unto his people; FOR HE SHALL NOT ENTER INTO THE LAND which I have given unto the children of Israel, because ye rebelled against my word at the water of Meribah. (NUMBERS 20:24)

73. And Moses stripped Aaron of his garments, and put them upon Eleazar his son, AND AARON DIED THERE IN THE TOP OF THE MOUNT: and Moses and Eleazar came down from the mount. (NUMBERS 20:28)

74. And the Lord sent fiery serpents among the people, and they bit the people; and much PEOPLE OF ISRAEL DIED. (NUMBERS 21:6)

75. And the Lord said unto Moses, make thee a fiery serpent and SET IT UPON A POLE; and it shall come to pass, that every one that is bitten, when he looketh upon it, SHALL LIVE And Moses made a serpent of brass and put it upon a pole, that if a serpent had bitten any, when he beheld the serpent of brass, HE LIVED. (NUMBERS 21:8-9)

76. The Israel sang this song, SPRING UP, O WELL, SING YE UNTO IT. (NUMBERS 21:17)

77. And the Lord said unto Moses, fear him not; FOR I HAVE DELIVERED HIM INTO THY HAND, and all his people, and his land, and thou shalt do to him as thou didst unto Sihon King of the Amorites, which dwelt at Heshbon. (NUMBERS 21:34)

78. Behold, there is a people come out of Egypt, which covereth the face of the earth: COME NOW, CURSE ME THEM; preadventure I shall be able to overcome them and DRIVE THEM OUT. (NUMBERS 22:11)

79. And Balaam rose up in the morning, and saddled his ass, and went with the princes of Moab. And God's anger was KINDLED BECAUSE HE WENT: and the angel of the Lord stood in the way for an adversary against him. Now he was riding upon his ass, and his two servants were with him. And the ass saw the ANGEL OF THE LORD STANDING IN THE WAY and his sword drawn in his hand; and the ass turned aside out of the way, and went into the field; AND BALAAM SMOTE THE ASS, TO TURN INTO THE WAY. (NUMBERS 22:21-23

80. And the ass saw me, and turned from me these three times unless she had turned from me, SURELY NOW ALSO I HAD SLAIN THEE, AND SAVED HER ALIVE. (NUMBERS 22:33)

81. How shall I curse, whom God hath NOT CURSE? Or how shall I defy, whom the Lord hath NOT DEFIED? (NUMBERS 23:8)

82. Behold, I have received commandment to bless: and he hath blessed: and I CANNOT REVERSE IT. (NUMBERS 23:20)

83. But Balaam answered and said unto Balak, told not I thee, saying, all that the Lord speaketh, THAT I MUST DO. (NUMBERS 23:26)

84. And Balaam lifted up his eyes, and he saw Israel abiding in his tents according to their tribes; AND THE SPIRIT OF GOD CAME UPON HIM. (NUMBERS 24:2)

85. And he took up his parable, and said, Balaam the son of Beor hath said, and the man whose eyes are open hath said; he hath said which heard the words of God, and knew THE KNOWLEDGE OF THE MOST HIGH. which saw the vision of the Almighty, FALLING INTO A TRANCE, but having his eyes open. (NUMBERS 24:15-16)

86. And he went after the man of Israel into the tent, and thrust both of them through, THE MAN OF ISRAEL, AND THE WOMAN THROUGH HER BELLY. So the plague was stayed from the children of Israel. And those that

died in the plague were TWENTY AND FOUR THOUSAND. (NUMBERS 25:8-9)

87. And it came to pass after the plague, that the Lord spake unto Moses and unto Eleazar the son of Aaron the priest saying, take the SUM OF ALL THE CONGREGATION of the children of Israel, from twenty years old and upward, throughout their father's house, all that are able to go to war in Israel. (NUMBERS 26:1-2)

88. And the Lord spake unto Moses, saying, unto these the land shall be divided FOR AN INHERITANCE according to the number of names. (NUMBERS 26:52-53)

89. But among these there WAS NOT A MAN whom Moses and Aaron the priest NUMBERED, when they numbered the children of Israel in the wilderness of Sinai. (NUMBERS 26:64)

90. And the Lord spake unto Moses, saying, the daughters of ZEKIOHEHAD SPEAK RIGHT: Thou shall surely give them a possession of an inheritance among their father's brethren; and thou shalt cause the inheritance OF THEIR FATHER TO PASS UNTO THEM. (NUMBERS 27:6-7)

91. And the Lord said unto MOSES, get thee up into this mount Abarim, AND SEE THE LAND which I have given unto the children of Israel. And when thou hast seen it, THOU ALSO SHALT BE GATHERED UNTO THY PEOPLE, as Aaron thy brother was gathered. (NUMBERS 27:12-13)

92. And Moses spake unto the Lord, saying, let the Lord, THE GOD OF THE SPIRIT OF ALL FLESH, set a man over the congregation. (NUMBERS 27:15-16)

93. And Moses did as the Lord commanded him: and he took JOSHUA, AND SET HIM BEFORE ELEAZAR THE PRIEST, and before all the congregation: and he LAID HIS HAND UPON HIM and gave him a charge as the Lord commanded by the hand of Moses. (NUMBERS 27:22-23)

94. And the Lord spake unto Moses, saying, command the children of Israel, and say unto them, MY OFFERING, AND MY BREAD FOR MY SACRIFICES MADE BY FIRE, for a sweet savour unto me, shall ye observe to offer unto me in their due season. (NUMBERS 28:1-2)

95. And a several tenth deal of flour mingled with oil for a meat offering unto one lamb; for a burnt offering of a sweet savour, SACRIFICE MADE BY FIRE UNTO THE LORD. (NUMBERS 28:13)

96. And in the seventh month, on the first day of the month, YE SHALL HAVE AN HOLY CONVOCATION; ye shall do no servile work; it is a day of blowing the trumpets unto you. (NUMBERS 29:1)

97. These things ye shall do unto the Lord in your set feasts, BESIDE YOUR VOWS AND YOUR FREEWILL OFFERINGS, for your burnt offerings, and for your meat offerings, and for your drink offerings, and for your peace offerings. (NUMBERS 29:39)

98. If a man vow a vow unto the Lord, or swear an oath to bind his soul with a bond; HE SHALL NOT BREAK HIS WORD, he shall do according to all that PROCEEDED OUT OF HIS MOUTH. (NUMBERS 30:2)

99. And they warred against the Midianites, as the Lord commanded Moses; AND THEY SLEW ALL THE MALES. (NUMBERS 31:7)

100. Everything that may abide in the fire, ye shall make it go through the fire, and it shall be clean NEVERTHELESS, IT SHALL BE PURIFIED WITH THE WATER OF SEPARATION; and all that abideth not the fire ye shall make go through the water. (NUMBERS 31:23)

101. And divide the prey into two parts; between them that took the war upon them, who went out to battle, and between all the CONGREGATION. (NUMBERS 31:27)

102. And Moses and Eleazar the priest took the gold of the captains of thousands and of hundrens, and brought it into the tabernacle of the congregation, FOR A MEMORIAL for the children of Israel before the Lord. (NUMBERS 31:54)

103. And the Lord's anger was kindled the same time, and he sware saying, surely none of the men that came up out of Egypt, from twenty years old and upward, shall see the land which I sware UNTO ABRAHAM, UNTO ISAAC AND UNTO JACOB; because they have not wholly followed me. Save CALEB the son of Jephunneh the Kenezite, AND JOSHUA the son of Nun; for they have WHOLLY FOLLOWED THE LORD. And the Lord's anger was kindled against Israel, And he made them wander in the wilderness FORTY YEARS, until all

the generation, that had done evil in the sight of the Lord, WAS CONSUMED. (NUMBERS 32:10-13)

104. And Moses said unto them, if the children of GAD and the children of REUBEN will pass with you OVER JORDAN , every man armed to battle, before the Lord, and the land shall be subdued before you; then ye shall give them the land of Gilead for a possession. (NUMBERS 32:29)

105. But if they will not pass over with you armed, they shall have possessions among you in the LAND OF CANAAN. (NUMBERS 32:30)

106. And Moses wrote their goings out according to their journeys by the commandment of the Lord; and these ARE THEIR JOURNEYS ACCORDING TO THEIR GOINGS OUT. (NUMBERS 33:2

107. Then ye shall drive out all the inhabitants of the land from before you, and destroy all their pictures, and destroy all their molten images, and quite pluck down ALL THEIR HIGH PLACES. (NUMBERS 33:52)

108. But if ye will not drive out the inhabitants of the land from before you; then it shall come to pass, that those which ye let remain of them shall be PRICKS IN YOUR EYES, AND THRONS IN YOUR SIDES, and shall vex you in the land wherein ye dwell. (NUMBERS 33:55)

109. And the Lord spake unto Moses, saying, command the children of Israel, and say unto them, when you come into THE LAND OF CANAAN; (this is the land that shall fall unto you for an inheritance, even the land of Canaan with the coast thereof). (NUMBERS 34:1-2)

110. These are the names of the men which shall divide the land unto you; ELEAZAR THE PRIEST AND JOSHUS THE SON OF DAN. (NUMBERS 34:17)

111. These are they whom the Lord commanded to divide the inheritance unto the children of Israel in the land of CANAAN. (NUMBERS 34:29)

112. And the suburbs of the cities, which ye shall give unto the LEVITES, shall reach from the wall of the city and outward a thousand cubit round about. (NUMBERS 35:4)

113. Ye shall give three cities on this side of Jordan, and three cities shall ye give in the land of Canaan, WHICH SHALL BE CITIES OF REFUGE. (NUMBERS 35:14)

114. Defile not therefore the land which ye shall inhabit, wherein I dwell: FOR I THE LORD DWELL AMONG the children of Israel. (NUMBERS 35:34)

115. This is the thing which the Lord doth command concerning the DAUGHTERS OF ZELOPHEHAD, saying, let them marry to whom they think best; only to the family of the tribe of their father SHALL THEY MARRY. (NUMBERS 36:6).

116.   These are the commandments and the judgments, which the Lord commanded by the hand of MOSES unto the children of Israel in the plains of Moah by Jordan near   JERICHO. (NUMBERS 36:13)

THE END NUMBERS

DEUTERONOMY

1. And it came to pass in the fortieth year, in the eleventh month, on the first day of the month, THAT MOSES SPAKE UNTO THE CHILDREN OF ISRAEL, according unto all that the Lord had given him in commandment unto them. (DEU. 1:3)

2. Behold, I have set the land before you: go in and possess the land which the Lord SWARE UNTO YOUR FATHER, Abraham, Isaac and Jacob to give unto them and to their seed after them. (DEU. 1:8)

3. Yet in this thing ye did not BELIEVE THE LORD YOUR GOD, who went in the way before you, to search you out a place to pitch your tent, IN FIRE BY NIGHT, to show you by what way ye should go, and IN A CLOUD BY DAY. (DEU. 1:32-33)

4. And the Lord said unto me, say unto them, GO NOT UP, neither fight; FOR I AM NOT AMONG YOUR ENEMIES lest ye be smitten before your enemies. (DEU. 1:42)

5. And the Amorites, which dwelt in that mountain, came out against you, AND CHASED YOU, AS BEES DO, and destroyed you in Seir, even unto Hormah. (DEU. 1:44)

6. Meddle not with them; for I will not give you of their land, no not so much as a foot breadth; BECAUSE I HAVE GIVEN MOUNT SEIR UNTO ESAU FOR A POSSESSION. DEU. 2:5)

7. For the Lord thy God hath BLESSED THEE in all the works of thy hand; he knoweth thy walking through this great wilderness; these forty years the Lord thy God hath been with thee; THOU HAST LACKED NOTHING. (DEU. 2:7)

8. For indeed the hand of the Lord was against them to destroy them from among the host, UNTIL THEY WERE CONSUMED. (DEU. 2:15)

9. And the Lord our God delivered him before us AND WE SMOTE HIM AND HIS SONS, and all his people. (DEU. 2:33)

10. So the Lord our God delivered into our hands Og also, the king of Bashan, and all his people; and we smote him until NONE WAS LEFT TO HIM REMAINING. (DEU. 3:3)

11. But charge JOSHUA, and encourage him, and strengthen him; for he shall go over before this people, AND HE SHALL CAUSE THEM TO INHERIT THE LAND which thou shalt see. (DEU. 3:28)

12. Ye shall not add unto the word which I command you, NEITHER SHALL YE DIMINISH AUGHT FROM IT, that ye may keep the commandments of the Lord your God which I command you. (DEU. 4:2)

13. Keep therefore and do them; for this is YOUR WISDOM AND YOUR UNDERSTANDING in the sight of the nation, which shall hear all these statutes, and say, surely this great nation is a wise and understanding people. (DEU. 4:6)

14. And he declared unto you his COVENANT which he commanded you to perform, even ten commandments and HE WROTE THEM UPON TWO TABLES OF STONES. (DEU. 4:13)

15. But I must die in this land, I MUST NOT GO OVER JORDAN but ye shall go over, and possess that good land. (DEU. 4:22)

16. But if from thence thou shalt seek the Lord thy God, thou shalt find him, IF THOU SEEK HIM WITH ALL THY HEART AND WITH ALL THY SOUL. (DEU. 4:29)

17. (for the Lord thy God is a merciful God) HE WILL NOT FORSAKE THEE, neither destroy thee, NOR FORGET THE COVENANT OF THY FATHERS, which he sware unto them. (DEU. 4:31)

18. Unto thee it was shown, that thou mightest know that the Lord he is God; THERE IS NONE ELSE BESIDE HIM. (DEU. 4:35)

19. And because he loved thy fathers, therefore he chose their seed after them, and brought thee out in his sight with MIGHTY POWER out of Egypt. (DEU. 4:37)

20. Know therefore, this day, and consider it in thine heart, that the Lord he is God IN HEAVEN ABOVE, and upon earth beneath. There is none other. (DEU. 4:39)

21. And Moses called all Israel, and said unto them, HEAR, O ISRAEL, the statutes and judgments which I speak in your ears this day, that ye may learn them, and keep and do them. The Lord our God made a COVENANT with us in Horeb. The Lord MADE NOT THIS COVENANT WITH OUR FATHERS, but with us. Even us, who are all of us here alive this day. (DEU. 5:1-3)

22. These words the Lord spake unto all your assembly in the mount out of the midst of the fire, of the cloud, and of the thick darkness, with a GREAT VOICE and he added no more. And he wrote them in TWO TABLES OF STONES, and delivered them unto me. (DEU. 5:22)

23. Ye shall walk in all the ways which the Lord your God hath commanded you, that ye may live, and that it may be well with you, AND THAT YE MAY PROLONG YOUR DAYS in the land which ye shall possess. (DEU. 5:33)

24. Hear therefore, O Israel, and observe to do it, that it may be well with thee AND THAT YE MAY INCREASE MIGHTLY, as the Lord God of thy fathers hath promised thee, IN THE LAND THAT FLOWETH WITH MILK AND HONEY, Hear O Israel; the Lord our God IS ONE LORD. And thou shall love the Lord thy God with all thine heart, and with all thy soul, and with all thy might. And these words, which I command thee this day shall be in thine heart . (DEU. 6:3-6)

25. And thou shall do that which is right and good IN THE SIGHT OF THE LORD: that it may be well with thee, and that thou mayest go in and possess the good land which the Lord sware unto my fathers. (DEU. 6:18)

26. For thou are an holy people unto the Lord thy God: the Lord thy God hath chosen thee to be a SPECIAL PEOPLE UNTO HIMSELF, above all people that are upon the face of the earth. (DEU. 7:6)

27. Know therefore that the Lord thy God, he is God, the faithful God which keepeth COVENANT AND MERCY with them that love him and keep his commandments TO A THOUSAND GENERATIONS. (DEU. 7:9)

28. And the Lord will take away from thee ALL SICKNESS, and will put none of the evil diseases of Egypt, which thou knowest, UPON THEE; but will lay them upon all them that HATE THEE. (DEU. 7:15)

29. And thou shalt REMEMBER all the way which the Lord thy God led thee these FORTY YEARS in the wilderness, TO HUMBLE THEE, AND TO PROVE THEE, to know what was in thine heart whether thou wouldest keep his commandments or no. (DEU. 8:2)

30. Therefore thou shalt keep the commandments of the Lord thy God, TO WALK IN HIS WAYS, AND TO FEAR HIM. (DEU.8:6)

31. But thou shalt remember the Lord thy God; FOR IT IS HE THAT GIVETH THEE POWER TO GET WEALTH, that he may establish his COVENANT which he sware unto thy fathers, AS IT IS THIS DAY. (DEU. 8:18)

32. And the Lord was very angry with AARON TO HAVE DESTROYED HIM; and I prayed for Aaron also the same time. And I took your sin, THE CALF WHICH YE HAD MADE and burnt it, and ground it very small, EVEN UNTIL IT WAS AS SMALL AS DUST and I cast the DUST thereof into the brook that descended out of the mount. (DEU. 9:20-21)

33. And he wrote on the tables, according to the first writing, THE TEN COMMANDMENTS, which the Lord spake unto you in the mount OUT OF THE MIDST OF THE FIRE in the day of the assembly: and the Lord gave them unto me. (DEU. 10:4)

34. Circumcise therefore the foreskin of your heart, AND BE NO MORE STIFFNECKED. (DEU. 10:16)

35. Love ye therefore the stranger : FOR YE WERE STRANGERS IN THE LAND OF EGYPT. (DEU. 10:19)

36. And what he did unto Dathan and Abiram, the sons of Eliab, the son of REUBEN: HOW THE EARTH OPENED HER MOUTH AND SWALLOWED THEM UP, and their households, and their tents, and all the substance that was in their possession, IN THE MIDST OF ALL ISRAEL. (DEU. 11:6)

37. Therefore shall ye lay up these my WORDS in your heart and in your soul, and bind them for a sign upon your hand, that THEY MAY BE AS FRONTLET BETWEEN YOUR EYES. (DEU. 11:18)

38. And ye shall observe to all the STATUTES AND JUDGEMENTS which I set before you this day. (DEU. 11:32)

39. And thither ye shall bring your BURNT OFFERING, and your SACRIFICES, and your TITHES, and HEAVE OFFERINGS of your hand and your VOWS and your FREEWILL OFFERING and the FIRSTLING of your herds and of your flocks. (DEU. 12:6)

40. Observe and hear all these words which I commend thee, that it may go well with thee, AND WITH THY CHILDREN AFTER THEE FOR EVER, when thou doest that which is good and right in the sight of the Lord thy God. (DEU. 12:28)

41. What thing soever I command you, observe to do it: THOU SHALT NOT ADD THERETO NOR DIMINISH FROM IT. (DEU. 12:32)

42. Thou shalt not hearken unto the words of THAT PROPHET OR THAT DREAMER OF DREAMS: for the Lord your God proveth you, to know whether ye love the Lord your God with all your heart and with all your soul. (DEU. 13:3)

43. And every beast that parteth the hoof, and cleaveth the cleft into two claws, and cheweth the cud among the beast, THAT YE SHALL EAT. (DEU. 14:6)

44. And every creeping thing that flieth is UNCLEAN unto you: THEY SHALL NOT BE EATEN. (DEU. 14:19)

45. At the end of EVERY SEVEN YEARS thou shalt make a RELEASE. (DEU. 15:1)

46. For the Lord thy God blesseth thee, as he promised thee: and THOU SHALL LEND UNTO MANY NATIONS, BUT THOU SHALL NOT BORROW; and thou shalt reign over many nations, BUT THEY SHALL NOT REIGN OVER THEE. (DEU. 15:6)

47. And when thou sendest him out free from thee, THOU SHALL NOT LET HIM GO AWAY EMPTY. (DEU. 15:13)

48. Observe the month of Abib, and keep the Passover unto the Lord thy God: for in the month of Abib the Lord thy God brought thee forth OUT OF EGYPT BY NIGHT. (DEU. 16:1)

49. Seven week shalt thou number unto thee; begin to number the seven weeks from such time as thou beginnest to PUT THE SICKLE TO THE CORN. (DEU. 16:9)

50. Thou shalt observe the feast of tabernacle SEVEN DAYS, after that thou hast gathered in thy corn and thy wine. (DEU. 16:13)

51. That which is ALTOGETHER JUST, shalt thou follow, that thou mayest live, and inherit the land which the Lord thy God giveth thee. (DEU. 16:20)

52. At the mouth of two witnesses, or three witnesses, shall he that is worthy of death be put to death; but at the mouth of one witness HE SHALL NOT BE PUT TO DEATH. (DEU. 17:6)

53. And it shall be, when he SITTETH UPON THE THRONE OF HIS KINGDOM, that he shall write him a copy of this law in a book out of that which is before the priest the Levites. (DEU. 17:18)

54. The Lord thy God will raise up unto thee A PROPHET FROM THE MIDST OF THEE, of thy brethren, like unto me, unto him ye shall hearken. (DEU. 18:15)

55. When a prophet speaketh in the name of the Lord, if the thing FOLLOW NOT, NOR COME TO PASS, that is the thing which the Lord hath NOT SPOKEN, but the prophet hath spoken it presumptuously; thou shalt not be afraid of him. (DEU. 18:22)

56. And those which remain shall hear, and fear, and shall henceforth commit NO MORE ANY SUCH EVIL AMONG YOU. (DEU. 19:20)

57. For the Lord thy God is he that goeth with you, to fight for you against your enemies, TO SAVE YOU. (DEU. 20:4)

58. If one be found slain in the land which the Lord thy God giveth thee to possess it, lying in the field, and it be not known WHO HATH SLAIN HIM. (DEU. 21:1)

59. And they shall answer and say, our hands have not shed this blood, NEITHER HAVE OUR EYES SEEN IT. (DEU. 21:7)

60. But he shall acknowledge the son of the hated for THE FIRSTBORN, BY GIVING HIM A DOUBLE PORTION OF ALL THAT HE HATH: for he is the beginning of his strength; the right of the firstborn is his. (DEU. 21:17)

61. The woman shall not wear that which pertained unto a man, neither shall a man put on a woman's garment: FOR ALL THAT DO SO ARE ABOMINATION UNTO THE LORD THY GOD. (DEU. 22:5)

62. A man shall not take his father's wife, NOR DISCOVER HIS FATHER'S SKIRT. (DEU. 22:30)

63. That which is gone out of thy lips thou shalt keep and perform; even a freewill offering, according as thou hast VOWED unto the Lord thy God, WHICH THOU HAST PROMISED WITH THY MOUTH. (DEU. 23:23)

64. Remember what the Lord thy God did unto MIRIAM by the way, after that ye were come forth out of Egypt. (DEU. 24:9)

65. The fathers shall not be put to death for the children, neither shall the children be put to death for the fathers: EVERY MAN SHALL BE PUT TO DEATH FOR HIS OWN SIN. (DEU. 24:16)

66. If there be a controversy between men, and they come unto judgement, that the judges may judge them; then they SHALL JUSTIFY THE RIGHTEOUS, AND CONDEMN THE WICKED. (DEU. 25:1)

67. And his name shall be called Israel, the house of him that HATH HIS SHOE LOOSED (DEU. 25:10)

68. That thou shalt take of the first of all the fruit of the earth, which thou shalt bring of thy land that the Lord thy God giveth thee, AND SHALT PUT IT IN A BASKET, and shalt go unto the place which the Lord thy God shall cooose to place his name there. (DEU.26:2)

69. And now, behold, I have brought the FIRSTFRUITS of the land, which thou, O LORD HAST GIVEN ME. And thou shalt set it before the Lord thy God and worship before the Lord thy God. (DEU:26:10)

70. When thou hast made an end of tithing all the tithes of thine increase the third year, WHICH IS THE YEAR OF TITHING, and hast given it unto the LEVITES, THE STRANGER, THE FATHERLESS AND THE WIDOW that they may eat within thy gates, and be filled. (DEU. 26:12)

71. Look down from thy holy habitation, from heaven, AND BLESS THY PEOPLE ISRAEL, and the land which thou hast given us, as thou swarest unto our fathers, A LAND THAT FLOWETH WITH MILK AND HONEY. (DEU. 26:15)

72. And Moses and the priests the Levites spake unto all Israel, saying, TAKE HEED, AND HEARKEN O ISRAEL; this day thou art become the people of the Lord thy God. Thou shall therefore OBEY THE VOICE OF THE LORD THY GOD, and do his commandments and his statutes, which I command thee this day. (DEU. 27:9-10)

73. Cursed be he that lieth with his FATHER'S WIFE; because he uncovered his father's SKIRT. And all the people shall say; AMEN. (DEU. 27:20)

74. And it shall come to pass, if thou shalt hearken diligently unto the VOICE of the Lord thy God to observe and to do all his commandments which I command thee this day, that the Lord thy God WILL SET THEE ON HIGH ABOVE ALL NATIONS OF THE EARTH: and all these blessing shall come on thee, AND OVERTAKE THEE if thou shalt hearken unto the VOICE of the Lord thy God. (DEU. 28:1-2)

75. Blessed shalt thou be when THOU COMEST IN and blessed shall thou be when THOU GOEST OUT. (DEU. 28:6)

76. The Lord shall cause thine enemies that rise up against thee to be smitten before thy face; they shall come out AGAINST THEE ONE WAY, AND FLEE BEFORE THEE SEVEN WAYS. (DEU. 28:7)

77. The Lord shall make thee the head, AND NOT THE TAIL; and thou shalt be ABOVE ONLY and thou shalt NOT BE BENEATH if that thou hearken

unto the commandments of the Lord thy God, which I command thee this day, to observe and TO DO THEM. (DEU. 28:13)

78. But it shall come to pass, if thou wilt NOT hearken unto the VOICE of the Lord thy God, to observe TO DO ALL his commandments and his statutes which I command thee this day; that all these CURSES SHALL COME UPON THEE, AND OVERTAKE THEE. (DEU. 28:15)

79. And ye shall be left few in number, whereas ye were AS THE STARS OF HEAVEN FOR MULTITUDE because thou wouldest not obey the VOICE of the Lord thy God. (DEU. 28:62)

80. These are the words of the covenant, which the Lord commanded Moses to make with the CHILDREN OF ISRAEL in the land of Moab, beside THE COVENANT WHICH HE MADE WITH THEM IN HOREB. (DEU. 29:1)

81. Keep therefore the words of this covenant, and do them, THAT YE MAY PROSPER IN ALL THAT YE DO. (DEU. 29:9)

82. The secret things belongs unto the Lord our God; BUT THOSE THINGS WHICH ARE REVEALED BELONG UNTO US and our children for ever, that we may do all the words of this law. (DEU. 29:29)

83. I call heaven and earth to record this day against you, that I have set before you life and death, blessing and curse: THEREFORE CHOOSE LIFE, THAT BOTH THOU AND THY SEED MAY LIVE. (DEU. 30:19)

84. That thou mayest love the Lord thy God, and that thou mayest OBEY HIS VOICE, and that thou mayest cleave unto him: FOR HE IS THY LIFE, AND THE LENGTH OF THY DAYS; that thou mayest dwell in the land which the Lord sware unto thy fathers, TO ABRAHAM, TO ISAAC, AND TO JACOB, to give them. (DEU. 30:20)

85. And Moses went and spake these words unto all Israel. And he said unto them, I am an hundred and twenty years old this day; I CAN NO MORE GO OUT AND COME IN; also the Lord hath said unto me, THOU SHALT NOT GO OVER THIS JORDAN. (DEU. 31:1-2.)

86. And Moses called unto Joshua, and said unto him in sight of all Israel, BE STRONG AND OF GOOD COURAGE; for thou must go with this people

unto the land which the Lord hath sworn unto their fathers to give them; AND THOU SHALL CAUSE THEM TO INHERIT IT . (DEU.31:7)

87. And the Lord said unto Moses, behold, thy days approach that thou MUST DIE: call JOSHUA and present yourselves in the tabernacle of the congregation, THAT I MAY GIVE HIM A CHARGE. And Moses and Joshua went, and presented themselves in the tabernacle of the congregation. (DEU. 31:14)

88. That Moses commanded the Levites, WHICH BARE THE ARK OF THE COVENANT of the Lord saying, take this book of the law and PUT IT IN THE SIDE OF THE ARK OF THE COVENANT of the Lord your God, that it may be there for a witness against thee. (DEU. 31:25-26)

89. Because I will publish the name of the Lord; ascribe ye GREATNESS UNTO OUR GOD. (DEU. 32:3)

90. Remember the days of old, consider the years of many generation; ask thy father, AND HE WILL SHOW THEE; thy elders and THEY WILL TELL THEE. (DEU. 32:7)

91. And Moses came and spake all the words of this song in the ears of the people, he, and Hoshea THE SON OF NUN. (DEU. 32:44)

92. And the Lord spake unto Moses that selfsame day, saying, get thee up into this mountain Abarim, UNTO MOUNT NEBO; which is in the land of Moah, THAT IS OVER AGAINST JERICHO; and behold the land of Canaan which I give unto the children of Israel for a possession. And DIE in the mount whither thou goest up, and be gathered unto thy people as Aaron thy brother DIED IN MOUNT HOR and was gathered unto his people. Because ye trespassed against me among the children of Israel at the waters of Meribah-Kadesh, IN THE WILDERNESS OF ZIN; because ye sanctified me not in the midst of the children of Israel. Yet thou shalt see the land before thee, BUT THOU SHALT NOT GO THITHER UNTO THE LAND which I give the children of Israel. (DEU. 32:48-52)

93. And this is the blessing, wherewith Moses the man of God blessed the children of Israel BEFORE HIS DEATH. (DEU. 33:1

94. And of Joseph he said, blessed of the Lord be his land for the PRECIOUS THINGS OF HEAVEN, for the dew, and for the deep that coucheth beneath. (DEU. 33:13)

95. And the Lord said unto him, this is the land which I sware unto Abraham, unto Isaac and unto Jacob, saying, I will give it unto thy seed; I have caused thee to see it with thine eyes, BUT THOU SHALT NOT GO OVER THITHER. SO MOSES THE SERVANT OF TH LORD DIED THERE IN THE LAND OF MOAH, according to the word of the Lord. (DEU. 34:4-5)

96. And Joshua the son Num was FULL OF THE SPIRIT OF WISDOM; for Moses had laid his hands upon him: AND THE CHILDREN OF ISRAEL hearkened unto him, and did as the Lord commanded Moses. (DEU. 34:9)

97. And there rose not a prophet since in Israel like unto MOSES, whom the Lord knew face to face. (DEU. 34:10)

The End DEUTERONOMY

THE NEW TESTAMENT
ST. MATTHEW

1. Abraham begat Isaac; and Isaac begat Jacob; and Jacob begat JUDAS AND ALL HIS BRETHREN. (MATT. 1:2)

2. And Jacob begat Joseph the husband of Mary, of whom was born JESUS who is called CHRIST. (MATT. 1:16)

3. So all the generation from Abraham to David are FOURTEEN GENERATIONS; and from David until the carrying away into Babylon are FOURTEEN GENERATIONS; and from the carrying away into Babylon unto Christ are FOURTEEN GENERATIONS. MATT. 1:17)

4. Now the birth of Jesus Christ was on this wise; when as his mother Mary was espoused to Joseph, before they came together, SHE WAS FOUND WITH CHILD OF THE HOLY GHOST. (MATT. 1:18)

5. Then Joseph her husband, BEING A JUST MAN, and not willing to make her public example, was minded to put her away privily. But while he thought on these things, behold, the angel of the Lord appeared unto him in a dream, saying, Joseph, THOU SON OF DAVID, fear not to take unto thee Mary thy wife; for that which is conceived in her IS OF THE HOLY GHOST. (MATT. 1:19-20)

6. Now all this was done, that it might be FULFILLED which was spoken of the Lord by the Prophet saying, Behold, a virgin shall be with child, and shall bring forth a son, and they shall call his name EMMANUEL, which being interpreted is, GOD WITH US. (MATT. 1:22-23)

7. And knew her not till she had brought forth her FIRSTBORN SON and he called his name JESUS. (MATT. 1:25)

8. Now when Jesus was born in BETHLEHEM of Judaea in the days of HEROD the king, behold, there came wise men FROM THE EAST to Jerusalem. (MATT. 2:1)

9. When Herod the king had heard these things, HE WAS TROUBLED and all Jerusalem with him. (MATT. 2:3)

10. And being warned of God in a dream that they should NOT RETURN TO HEROD; they DEPARTED into their own country ANOTHER WAY. (MATT. 2:12)

11. And when they were departed, behold, THE ANGEL OF THE LORD appeared to Joseph in a DREAM, saying, arise, and take the young child and his mother and flee into Egypt, and be thou there until I bring thee word; for Herod will seek the young child TO DESTROY HIM. (MATT. 2:13)

12. But when Herod was dead, behold, an angel of the Lord apeareth in a dream to JOSEPH IN EGYPT. Saying, arise, and take the young child and his mother and go into the land of Israel; for they are dead which sought THE YOUNG CHILD'S LIFE. (MATT. 2:19-20)

13. But when he heard that Archelaus did reign in Judaea in the room of his father Herod, he was afraid to go thither; notwithstanding BEING WARNED OF GOD IN A DREAM, he turned aside into the parts of Galilee. And he came and dwelt in a city called NAZARETH; that it might be fulfilled which was spoken by the prophets, He shall be called a NAZARENE. (MATT. 2:22-23)

14. In those days came John the Baptist PREACHING in the wilderness of JUDAEA. (MATT. 3:1)

15. For this is he that was spoken of by the Prophet Esaias, saying, THE VOICE OF ONE CRYING IN THE WILDERNESS, prepare ye the way of the Lord, make his path straight. (MATT. 3:3)

16. And the same John had his raiment of camel's hair, and a leathern girdle about his loins; and his meat was LOCUSTS AND WILD HONEY. (MATT. 3:4)

17. I indeed baptize you with water unto repentance: but he that cometh after me is MIGHTIER THAN I, whose shoes I am not worthy to bear; he shall baptize you with the HOLY GHOST AND WITH FIRE. (MATT. 3:11)

18. Then cometh Jesus from Galilee to Jordan unto John to be BAPTIZED of him. (MATT. 3:13)

19. And Jesus, when he was baptized, went up straightway out of the water; and , LO, THE HEAVENS WERE OPENED UNTO HIM, and he saw the Spirit of

God descending LIKE A DOVE, AND LIGHTING UPON HIM. And lo a voice from heaven, saying, this is my beloved Son, IN WHOM I AM WELL PLEASED. (MATT. 3:16-17)

20. Then was Jesus led up of the Spirit into the wilderness to be tempted of the devil. And when he had fasted FORTY DAYS and FORTY NIGHTS, he was afterward an hungered. (Matt. 4:1-2)

21. Jesus said unto him, it is written again, THOU SHALL NOT TEMPT the Lord thy God. (MATT. 4:7).

22. Then saith Jesus unto him, Get thee hence, Satan: for it is written, THOU SHALT WORSHIP THE LORD THY GOD, and him only shalt thou serve. (MATT. 4:10)

23. Then the devil leaveth him, and behold, angels came and MINISTERED UNTO HIM. (MATT. 4:11)

24. Now when Jesus had heard that John was CAST, INTO PRISON he departed into GALILEE. (MATT. 4:12)

25. From that time Jesus began to preach, and to say, REPENT; for the kingdom of heaven is at hand. (MATT. 4:17)

26. And he saith unto them, FOLLOW ME, and I will make you fishers of men. (MATT. 4:19)

27. And going on from thence, he saw other two brethren, James the son of Zebedee, and John his brother, in a ship with Zebedee their father, mending their nets; and he called them. And they IMMEDIATELY left the ship and their father and FOLLOWED HIM. (MATT. 4:21-22)

28. And Jesus went about all Galilee, teaching in their synagogues and preaching the gospel of the kingdom, and HEALNG all manner of sickness and all manner of DISEASE among the people. (MATT. 4:23)

29. And seeing the multitudes, he went up into a MOUNTAIN; and when he was set, his DISCIPLES came unto him: and he opened his mouth, and taught them, saying, (MATT. 5:1-2)

30. Blessed are the poor in spirit; for theirs is the KINGDOM OF HEAVEN. (MATT. 5:3)

31. Blessed are the merciful; for they shall obtain MERCY. (MATT. 5:7)

32. Blessed are ye, when men shall revile you and persecute you, and shall say all MANNER OF EVIL AGAINST YOU FALSELY, for my sake. (MATT. 5:11)

33. Verse 16 notes, Let your light so shine before men, that they may see your good works, and GLORIFY your father which is in heaven. (MATT. 5:16)

34. Verse 22 says… but whosoever shall say, thou fool, shall be in danger of hell fire. (MATT. 5:22)

35. Verse 34 notes, But I say unto you, swear not at all; neither by heaven; for it is GOD'S THRONE. (MATT. 5:34)

36. That ye may be the children of your Father which is in heaven; for he MAKETH HIS SUN TO RISE ON THE EVIL and on the good, and sendeth rain on the JUST AND ON THE UNJUST. (MATT. 5:45)

37. Verses 9-13 entails "The Lord's Prayer". (MATT. 6:9-13)

38. No man can serve two masters; for either he will hate the one, and love the other; or else he will hold to the one, and despise the other. YE CANNOT SERVE GOD AND MAMMON. (MATT. 6:24)

39. But SEEK ye first the kingdom of God, and his RIGHTEOUSNESS; and all these things shall be ADDED unto you. (MATT. 6:33)

40. Judge NOT, that ye be not judged. (MATT 7:1)

41. Ask, and it shall be GIVEN you, SEEK,. and ye shall find; KNOCK, and it shall be opened unto you . (MATT. 7:7)

42. Beware of false prophets, which come to you in sheep's clothing, but inwardly they are RAVENING WOLVES. (MATT. 7:15)

43. Wherefore by their FRUITS ye shall know them.(MATT. 7:20)

44. And the rain descended, and the FLOODS CAME. And the WINDS BLEW, and beat upon that house; and IT FELL; and great was the fall of it. (MATT. 7:27)

45. And Jesus said unto the Centurion, go thy way; and as thou hast BELIEVED, so be it done unto thee. And his servant was healed in the SELFSAME HOUR. (MATT. 8:13)

46. And when he was entered into a ship, his disciples FOLLED HIM and behold, there arose a great TEMPEST IN THE SEA, insomuch that the ship was COVERED WITH THE WAVES; but he was asleep. And his disciples came to him, and awoke him, saying, LORD, SAVE US: WE PERISH. And he saith unto them, why are ye fearful, O YE OF LITTLE FAITH. Then he arose, and rebuked the winds and the sea; and there was a GREAT CALM. But the men marveled, saying, WHAT MANNER OF MAN IS THIS, that even the winds and the sea OBEY HIM! (MATT. 8:23-27)

47. And, behold, they brought to him a man sick of the palsy, lying on a bed; and Jesus SEEING THEIR FAITH said unto the sick of the palsy; son, be of good cheer; THY SINS BE FORGIVEN THEE. (MATT. 9:2)

48. And as Jesus passed forth from thence, he saw a man called MATTHEW, sitting at the receipt of custom: and he said unto him FOLLOW ME and he arose, and FOLLOWED HIM. (MATT. 9:9)

49. But go ye and learn what that meaneth, I will have mercy, and not sacrifice: for I AM not come to call the righteousness, BUT SINNERS TO REPENTANCE. (MATT. 9:13)

50. While he spake these things unto them, behold, THERE CAME A CERTAIN RULER, and worship him, saying, my daughter is even NOW DEAD but come and lay thou hand upon her, and SHE SHALL LIVE. And Jesus arose, and followed him, and so did his disciples. And behold, a woman, which was diseased with AN ISSUE OF BLOOD TWELVE YEARS came behind him, and touched the hem of his garment: for she said within herself, if I may touch his garment, I shall be whole. But Jesus turned him about, and when he saw her, he said, daughter, be of good comfort; THY FAITH HATH MADE THEE WHOLE. And the woman was made whole from that hour. (MATT 9:18-22)

51. And when Jesus came into the ruler's house, and saw the minstrels and the people making a noise. He said unto them, give place, for the maid is not dead, BUT SLEEPETH. And they laughed him to scorn. But when the people were put forth, he went in and took her by the hand, AND THE MAID AROSE. (MATT. 9:23-25)

52. And the fame hereof went aboard into ALL THE LAND. (MATT. 9:26)

53. And when he was come into the house, THE BLIND MAN came to him; and Jesus saith unto them, BELIEVE YE THAT I AM ABLE TO DO THIS? They said unto him yea Lord. Then TOUCHED he their eyes saying, ACCORDING TO YOUR FAITH be it unto you. And their eyes were OPENED; And Jesus straitly charged them saying, see that no man know this. (MATT. 9:28-30)

54. As they went out, behold, they brought to him a DUMB MAN possessed with a devil. And when the devil was cast out, THE DUMB MAN SPAKE; and the multitudes marveled, saying, it was never so seen in Israel. (MATT. 9:32-33)

55. And when Jesus had called unto him his twelve disciples, he gave THEM POWER against unclean spirits, to cast them out, and to HEAL ALL MANNER OF SICKNESS AND ALL MANNER OF DISEASE. (MATT. 10:1)

56. Now the names of the twelve apostles are these: (MATT. 10:2-4)

1. (a) PETER	7. (g) THOMAS
2. (b) ANDREW	8. (h) MATTHEW
3. (c) JAMES	9. (I) JAMES
4. (d) JOHN	10. (j) LEBBAEUS
5. (e) PHILIP	11. (k) SIMON
6. (f) BARTHOLOMEW	12. (l) JUDAS ISCARIOT

57. And as ye go, PREACH, saying, the kingdom of heaven is at hand. Heal the sick, cleanse the lepers, and raise the dead, cast out devils: FREELY YE HAVE RECEIVED, FREELY GIVE. (MATT. 10:7-8)

58. And whosoever shall not receive you, nor hear your words, when ye depart out of that house or city, SHAKE OFF THE DUST OF YOUR FEET. (MATT. 10:14)

59. But when they deliver you up, take NO THOUGHT how or what ye shall speak; for it shall BE GIVEN you in that same hour what ye shall speak. (MATT. 10:19)

60. For it is not ye that speak, but the SPIRIT OF YOUR FATHER which speaketh IN YOU. (MATT. 10:20)

61. Fear them not therefore; for there is NOTHING COVERED, that shall not be REVEALED; and hid, that shall not BE KNOWN. (MATT.10:26)

62. He that receiveth you receiveth me, and he that receiveth me RECEIVETH HIM THAT SENT ME. (MATT. 10:40)

63. And it came to pass, when Jesus had made an end of commanding his TWELVE DISCIPLES, he departed thence to TEACH and to PREACH in their cities. (MATT. 11:1)

64. Now when John had heard in the prison the works of Christ, he sent TWO OF HIS DISCIPLES. (MATT. 11:2)

65. And as they departed, Jesus began to say unto the multitudes CONCERNING JOHN,   what went ye out into the wilderness to see? A reed shaken with the wind? (MATT. 7:11)

66. For this is he, of whom it is written, behold, I send my MESSENGER before thy face, which shall PREPARE thy way before thee. (MATT. 11:10)

67. And from the days of JOHN THE BAPTIST until now the kingdom of heaven suffered violence, and the violent take it by force. (MATT. 11:12)

68. For all the prophets and the law PROPHESIED until JOHN. (MATT. 11:13)

69. For my yoke is easy, and MY BURDEN IS LIGHT (MATT. 11:30).

70. And behold, there was a man which had his hand withered. And they asked him, saying, IS IT LAWFUR TO HEAL ON THE SABBATH DAY? That they might accuse him. And he said unto them, what man shall there be among you, that shall have one sheep, and IF IT FALL INTO A PIT ON THE SABBATH DAY, will he not lay hold on it, and lift it out? How much then is a man better than a sheep? Wherefore, IT IS LAWFUL TO DO WELL ON THE SABBATH

DAYS. Then said he to the man, STRETCH FORTH THINE HAND. And he stretched it forth; and it was stored whole, like as the other. (MATT. 12:10-13)

71 He that is not with me is AGAINST ME; and he that GATHERED NOT with me scattered abroad. (MATT. 12:30).

72. Therefore I say unto you, all manner of sin and blasphemy SHALL BE FORGIVEN unto men: but the blasphemy AGAINST THE HOLY GHOST shall not be forgiven unto men. (MATT. 12:13)

73. But I say unto you, that EVERY IDLE WORD that men shall speak, they SHALL GIVE ACCOUNT THEREOF in the day of judgement. (MATT. 12:36)

74. And he spake many things unto them in PARABLES, saying, behold, a sower went forth to sow; and when he sowed, some seeds FELL BY THE WAY SIDE, and the fowls came and devoured them up. (MATT. 13:3-4)

75. The sower sowed seeds in four different places; BY THE WAY SIDE, STONY PLACES, AMONG THORNS and GOOD GROUND. (MATT. 13:4-8)

76. But he that received seed into the GOOD GROUND is he that heareth the word, and understand it; which also beareth fruit, and bringeth forth, some an HUNDREDFOLD, some SIXTY, some THIRTY. (MATT. 13:23)

77. Let both grow together until the harvest; and in the time of harvest I will say to the reaper, GATHER YE TOGETHER, FIRST THE TARES, and bind them in bundles to burn them; but gather the wheat into my barn. (MATT. 13:30)

78. Then Jesus sent the multitude away, and went into the house; and his DISCIPLES came unto him, saying, declare unto us the PARABLE of the tares of the field. He answered and said unto them, he that soweth the good seed is the SON OF MAN; the field is THE WORLD; the good seed are the children of the KINGDOM; but the tares are the children of the WICKED ONE. The enemy that sowed them is THE DEVIL; the harvest is the END OF THE WORLD; and the reapers are THE ANGLES. (MATT. 13:36-39)

79. So shall it be at the end of the WORLD; the angels shall come forth, and SEVER THE WICKED FROM AMONG THE JUST. (MATT. 13:49)

80. For John said unto him, it is NOT LAWFUL for thee to have HER. (MATT. 14:4)

81. And he sent, and BEHEADED John in the PRISON. (MATT. 14:10)

82. And he commanded the multitude to sit down on the grass, and TOOK THE FIVE LOAVES and the TWO FISHES, and looking up to heaven, he blessed, and brake, and gave the loaves to his DISCIPLES, and the disciples to the multitude. And they did all eat and were filled; and they took up of the fragments that remained TWELVE BASKET full. And they that had eaten were about FIVE THOUSAND MEN beside women and children. (MATT. 14:19-21)

83. And in the fourth watch of the night Jesus went unto them, WALKING ON THE SEA. And when the disciples saw him walking on the sea, they were troubled, saying IT IS A SPIRIT; and they cried out for fear. But straightway Jesus spake unto them, saying, be of good cheer; IT IS I, be not afraid. And Peter answered him and said, Lord, if it be thou, bid me to COME unto thee on the water. And he said, COME. And when Peter was come down out of the ship, he walked on the water, to go to Jesus. But when he saw the wind boisterous, he was AFRAID; and beginning to sink, he cried, saying, Lord, save me. And IMMEDIATELY Jesus stretched forth his hand, and caught him, and said unto him, O thou of little FAITH, wherefore didst thou doubt? (MATT. 14:25-31)

84. And besought him that they might only TOUCH the hem of his garment; as many as touched WERE MADE PERFECTLY WHOLE. (MATT. 14:36)

85. Not that which goeth into the mouth defileth a man; but that which cometh out of THE MOUTH, this defileth a man. (MATT. 15:11)

86. Do not ye yet understand, that whatsoever entereth in at the mouth goeth into the belly, and is cast out into the draught? But those things which PROCEED OUT OF THE MOUTH come forth FROM THE HEART; and they defile the man. For out of THE HEART proceed evil thoughts, murders, adulteries, fornications, thefts, false witness, blasphemies; these are the things which DEFILE A MAN; but to eat with unwashen hands defileth NOT a man. (MATT. 15:18-20)

87. Then Jesus answered and said unto her, O woman, GREAT IS THY FAITH; be it unto thee even as thou wilt. And her daughter was made whole from that very hour. (MATT. 15:28)

88. And they said, some say thou art JOHN THE BAPTIST; some, ELIAS; and others, JEREMIAS, or one of the prophets. He saith unto them, but whom say ye that I AM ? (MATT. 16:14-16)

89. For the Son of man shall come in the glory of his Father WITH HIS ANGELS; and then he SHALL REWARD EVERY MAN according to his works. (MATT. 16:27)

90. While he yet spake, behold a bright cloud overshadowed them: and behold a voice out of the cloud, which said, this is my beloved Son, in whom I am well pleased; HEAR YE HIM. (MATT. 17:5)

91. And while they abode in Galilee, Jesus said unto them, The Son of man shall be BETRAYED into the hands of men: and they shall KILL HIM, and the THIRD DAY he shall be RAISED AGAIN. And they were exceeding sorry. (MATT. 17:22-23)

92. For the Son of man is come to save that which was lost. How think ye? If a man have an hundred sheep, and one of them be gone astray, doth he not leave the NINETY AND NINE, and goeth into the mountains, and seeketh that which is gone astray? And if so be that he find it, verily I say unto you, he rejoiceth more of THAT sheep, than of the ninety and nine which went not astray. (MATT. 18:12-13)

93. Again I say unto you, that if two of you shall agree on earth as TOUCHING ANY THING that they shall ask, it shall be done for them of my father which is in heaven. For where TWO OR THREE are gathered together in my name, there am I in the MIDST of them. (MATT. 18:19-20)

94. Then came Peter to him and said, Lord, how oft shall my brother sin against me and I forgive him? Till seven times? Jesus saith unto him I say not unto thee, Until seven times; but Until SEVENTY TIMES SEVEN. (MATT. 18:21-22

95. And again I say unto you, it is easier for a camel to go through THE EYE OF A NEEDLE, than for a rich man to enter into the KINGDOM OF GOD. (MATT. 19:24)

96. So the last shall be first, and first last: for many be called but FEW CHOSEN. (MATT. 20:16)

97. Even as the Son of man came not to be ministered unto, BUT TO MINISTER, and to give his life a ransom FOR MANY. (MATT. 20:28)

98. So Jesus had COMPASSION on them, and touched their eyes: and immediately their eyes received sight, and they FOLLOWED HIM. (MATT. 20:34)

99. Jesus sent two disciples saying unto them, go into the village over against you, and straightway ye shall find an ass tired and a colt with her LOOSE THEM, and bring them unto me. And if any man say aught unto you ye shall say, THE LORD HAST NEED OF THEM; and straightway he will send them, all this was done that it might be fulfilled which was spoken by the prophet saying, TELL YE THE DAUGHTER OF ZION, BEHOLD, thy king cometh unto thee, meek, and sitting upon an ass. (MATT. 21:1-5)

100. And Jesus went into the temple of God, and CAST OUT all them that sold and brought in the temple, and overthrew the TABLE OF THE MONEYCHANGERS, and the seats of them that sold doves. And said unto them, it is written, my house shall be called the HOUSE OF PRAYER, but ye have made it a den of thieves. (MATT. 21:13-14)

101. And when he saw a fig tree in the way, he came to it, and found nothing thereon, but leaves only, and said unto it, let no fruit grow in thee henceforward FOR EVER. And presently the fig tree withered away. And when the disciples saw it, they marvelled, saying, how soon is the fig tree withered away! Jesus answered and said unto them, Verily I say unto you, if ye have FAITH, and DOUBT NOT, ye shall not only do this which is done to the fig tree, but also if ye shall say unto this mountain, BE THOU REMOVED, and be thou cast into the sea; IT SHALL BE DONE. And all things, whatsoever ye shall ask in prayer BELIEVING, ye shall receive. (MATT. 21:19-22)

102. They say unto him, Caesar's. Then saith he unto them, Render therefore unto Caesar the things which are Caesar's; and unto God the THINGS THAT ARE GOD'S. (MATT. 22:21)

103. Now there were with us seven brethren; and the first, when he had married a wife, deceased, and having no issue, LEFT HIS WIFE UNTO HIS BROTHER.

Likewise the second also, and the third unto the SEVENTH. And last of all the woman died also. Therefore in the resurrection whose wife shall she be of the seven? For they all had her. Jesus answered and said unto them, YE DO ERR, not knowing the scriptures, nor the POWER OF GOD. For in the resurrection they NEITHER MARRY NOR ARE GIVEN IN MARRIAGE, but are as the angels of God in heaven. (MATT. 22:25-30)

104. Master, which is the great commandment in the law? Jesus said unto him, Thou shalt love THE LORD THY GOD with all thy heart, and with all thy soul, and with all thy mind. This is the first and great commandment. And the second is like unto it Thou shalt LOVE THY NEIGHBOR AS THYSELF. On these two commandments HANG all the law and the prophets. (MATT. 22:36-40)

105. And call no man your father upon the earth; for one is your father, WHICH IS IN HEAVEN. (MATT. 23:9)

106. For I say unto you, ye shall not see me henceforth, till ye shall say, BLESSED IS HE that cometh in the name of the Lord. (MATT. 23:39)

107. And as he sat upon the mount of Olives, the discipled came unto him privately, saying, TELL US WHEN SHALL THESE THINGS BE? And what SHALL BE the signs of thy coming, and of the end of the world? (MATT. 24:3)

108. And ye shall hear of wars and rumours of wars: SEE THAT YE BE NOT TROUBLED; for all these things must come to pass, but the END IS NOT YET COME. (MATT. 24:6)

109. But he that shall endure unto the end, THE SAME SHALL BE SAVED. (MATT. 24:13)

110. And this gospel of the kingdom shall be preached in ALL THE WORLD for a witness unto all nations; AND THEN SHALL THE END COME. (MATT. 24:14)

111. For as the lightning cometh out of the EAST, and shineth even unto the WEST; so shall also the coming of the Son of man be. (MATT. 24:27)

112. And then shall appear the sign of the Son of man in heaven; and then shall all the TRIBES of the earth mourn, and they shall see the Son of man coming

in the CLOUDS OF HEAVEN with power and GREAT GLORY. (MATT. 24:30)

113. Heaven and earth shall pass away, but my words SHALL NOT PASS AWAY (MATT. 24:35)

114. And knew not until the flood came, and took them all away; so shall also the COMING of the Son of man be. (MATT. 24:39)

115. Watch therefore; for ye know not WHAT HOUR your Lord doth come. (MATT: 24:42)

116. And the foolish said unto the wise, give us of your oil; for our lamps are GONE OUT. But the wise answered, saying, not so; lest there be not enough for us and you; but rather to them that sell, AND BUY FOR YOURSELVES. And while they went to buy, the BRIDEGROOM COME; and they that were ready went in with him to the marriage; and THE DOOR WAS SHUT. Afterward came also the other virgins, saying, Lord, LORD, OPEN TO US. (MATT. 25:8-11)

117. His lord said unto him, well done, thou good and faithful servant; thou hast been FAITHFUL over a few things, I will make thee RULER over many things; enter thou into THE JOY OF THY LORD. (MATT. 25:21)

118. And these shall go away into EVERLASTING punishment; but the righteous into LIFE ETERNAL. (MATT. 25:46)

119. And it came to pass, when Jesus had finished all these sayings, he said unto his disciples; ye know that after two days is the feast of the PASSOVER, and the Son of man is betrayed to be CRUCIFIED. There came a woman having an alabaster box of VERY PRECIOUS OINTMENT, and poured it on his head, as he sat at meat. But when his disciples saw it, they had indignation, saying, TO WHAT PURPOSE IS THIS WASTE? Verily, I say unto you WHERESOEVER this gospel shall be PREACHED in the whole world, there shall also this, that this woman hath done, BE TOLD FOR A MEMORIAL OF HER. Then one of the twelve, called JUDAS ISCARIOT, went unto the chief priests, and said unto them, what will ye give me, and I will deliver him unto you? And they COVENANTED with him for THIRTY PIECES OF SILVER. (MATT. 26:1-15)

120. And as they did eat, he said, Verily I say unto you that one of you SHALL BETRAY ME. (MATT 26:21)

121. And as they were eating, Jesus took bread, and BLESSED IT, and brake it and gave it to the disciples, and said, take, eat, this is MY BODY. And he took the cup, and GAVE THANKS, and gave it to them, saying, drink ye ALL OF IT. (MATT. 26:26-27)

122. Jesus said unto him, verily I say unto thee, that this night, before the cock crow, thou shall DENY ME THRICE. (MATT. 26:34)

123. And while he yet spake, lo, Judas, one of the twelve, came, and with him a GREAT MULTITUDE with swords and staves, from the chief priests and elders of the people. Now he that betrayed him gave them a sign, saying, WHOSOEVER I SHALL KISS, that same is he; hold him fast. And forthwith he came to Jesus, and said, Hail, master; and kissed him. (MATT. 26:47-49)

124. And after a while came unto him they that stood by, and said to Peter, surely thou also art one of them; FOR THY SPEECH BETRAYED THEE. Then began he to CURSE AND TO SWEAR, saying, I know not the man. And immediately the COCK CREW. And Peter remembered the WORD OF JESUS, which said unto him before the cock crow, thou shall deny me thrice. And he went out and WEPT BITTERLY. (MATT. 26:73-75)

125. When the morning was come, all the chief priest and elders of the people took counsel against Jesus to put him to DEATH. And when they had bound him, they led him away, and delivered him to Pontius Pilate, THE GOVERNOR. Then Judas, which had betrayed him, when he saw that he was CONDEMNED, REPENTED HIMSELF, and brought again the thirty pieces of silver to the chief priest and elders, saying I have sinned in that I have betrayed THE INNOCENT BLOOD. And they said, what is that to us? See thou to that. And he casted down the pieces of silver in the temple, and departed and went and HANGED HIMSELF. (MATT. 27:1-5)

126. When Pilate saw that he could prevail nothing, but that rather a tumult was made, he TOOK WATER, AND WASHED HIS HANDS, before the multitude saying, I am innocent of the blood of this JUST PERSON; see ye to it. (MATT. 27:24)

127. Now from the SIXTH HOUR there was darkness over all the land unto the NINETH HOUR. (MATT. 27:45)

128. And about the ninth hour Jesus cried with a loud voice, saying, Eli, Eli lama sabachthan? That is to say, MY GOD, WHY HAST THOU FORSAKEN ME? (MATT. 27:46)

129. Jesus, when he had cried again with a loud voice, YIELDED UP THE GHOST. (MATT. 27:50)

130. And the angel answered and said unto the women, fear not ye; for I know that ye SEEK JESUS, which was crucified. HE IS NOT HERE: FOR HE IS RISEN, as he said. Come, see the place where the Lord lay. (MATT. 28:5-6)

131. And as they went to tell his disciples, behold, Jesus met them, saying, ALL HAIL. And they came and held him by the feet, and worshipped him. Then said Jesus unto them, Be not afraid; go tell my brethren that they go into Galilee, AND THERE SHALL THEY SEE ME. (MATT. 28:9-10)

132. Then the eleven disciples went away into Galilee, into a mountain where Jesus HAD APPOINTED THEM. And when they saw him, they worshipped him: BUT SOME DOUBLED. (MATT. 28:16-17)

133. And Jesus came and spake unto them, saying, ALL POWER IS GIVEN UNTO ME IN HEAVEN AND IN EARTH. Go ye therefore, and teach all nations, BAPTIZING them in the name of the Father, and of the Son, and of the Holy Ghost: Teaching them to observe all things WHATSOEVER I have commanded you; and, lo, I AM WITH YOU ALWAYS, EVEN UNTO THE END OF THE WORLD. AMEN. (MATT. 28:18-20)

THE END ST. MATTEW

ST. MARK

1. The beginning of the gospel of Jesus Christ, the son of God; as it is written in the prophets: BEHOLD, I SEND MY MESSENGER before thy face, which shall prepare thy way before thee. (MARK. 1:1-2)

2. The voice of one crying in the wilderness, PREPARE YE THE WAY OF THE LORD, make his path straight. (MARK. 1:3)

3. John did baptize in the wilderness, and preached the baptism of REPENTANCE FOR THE REMISSION OF SINS. (MARK 1:4)

4. And preached, saying, there cometh ONE MIGHTIER THAN I after me, the latchet of whose shoes I am not worthy to STOOP DOWN AND UNLOOSE. (MARK 1:7)

5. I indeed have baptized you with water; but he shall baptize you WITH THE HOLY GHOST. (MARK 1:8)

6. And it came to pass in those days, that Jesus came from Nazareth of Galilee, and was baptized of in JORDAN. And straightway coming up out of the water, he saw the HEAVENS OPENED AND THE SPIRIT LIKE A DOVE descending upon him. And there came a voice from heaven , saying, THOU ART MY BELOVED SON, in whom I am well pleased. And immediately the Spirit driveth him in the WILDERNESS. And he was there in the wilderness FORTY DAYS, tempted of SATAN; and was with the wild beasts; and the angel ministered unto him. Now after that John was PUT IN PRISON, Jesus came into Galilee, PREACHING THE GOSPEL of the kingdom of God. (MARK. 1:9-14)

7. And saying, the time is fulfilled, and the kingdom of God is at hand: REPENT YE AND BELIEVE THE GOSPEL. (MARK. 1:15)

8. Now as he walked by the sea of GALILEE, he saw Simon and Andrew his brother casting a net into the sea; for they were fishers. And Jesus said unto them, COME YE AFTER ME, and I will make you TO BECOME FISHERS OF MEN. And straightway they forsook their nets and FOLLOWED HIM. (MARK. 1:16)

9. And there was in their synagogue a man with an UNCLEAN SPIRIT and he cried out, saying, LET US ALONE; what have we to do with thee, thou Jesus

of Nazareth? Art thou come to destroy us? I KNOW THEE who thou art, the Holy One of God. And Jesus rebuked him, saying, HOLD THY PEACE AND COME OUT OF HIM. And when the unclean spirit HAD TORN HIM, and cried with a loud voice, he came out of him. (MARK. 1:23-26)

10. And Jesus moved with COMPASSION , put forth his hand, and touched him, and saith unto him, I WILL; BE THOU CLEAN. (MARK 1:41)

11. And saith unto him, see thou say nothing to any man; but go thy way, SHOW THYSELF TO THE PRIEST. And offer for thy cleansing those things which Moses commanded FOR A TESTIMONY UNTO THEM. (MARK 1:44)

12. And when they could not come nigh unto him for the press, they UNCOVERED THE ROOF where he was; and when they had broken it up, they let down the bed wherein THE SICK OF THE PALSY LAY, when Jesus saw THEIR FAITH, he said unto the sick of the palsy, son thy sins be forgiven thee. (MARK 2:4-5)

13. And immediately when Jesus PRECEIVED IN HIS SPIRIT that they so reasoned within themselves, he said unto them, why reason ye these things in your HEARTS? Whether is it easier to say to the sick of the palsy, thy sins be forgiven thee; or to say, Arise, and take up thy bed, and walk? But that ye may know that the SON OF MAN hast power on earth to FORGIVE SINS (he saith to the sick of the palsy) I say unto thee, arise, and TAKE UP THY BED, and go thy way into thine house. And IMMEDIATELY he arose, took up the bed, and went forth before them all; insomuch that they were all amazed, and glorified God, saying, we never saw it on this fashion. (MARK 2:8-12)

14. When Jesus heard it, he saith unto them: they that are WHOLE have no need of the PHYSICIAN, but they that are sick: I came not to call the righteous, but SINNERS TO REPENTANCE. (MARK 2:17)

15. And he said unto them, the SABBATH was made for man, and not man for the SABBATH; Therefore, the Son of man is Lord also of the SABBATH. (MARK 2:27-28)

16. And they watched him, whether he would heal him on the Sabbath day that they MIGHT ACCUSE HIM. (MARK 3:2)

17. And when he had looked round about on them with anger, being grieved for the HARDNESS OF THEIR HEARTS, he saith unto the man, stretch forth

thine hand. And his hand was RESTORED WHOLE as the other. (MARK 3:5)

18. And unclean spirits, when they saw him FELL DOWN BEFORE HIM, and cried, saying, thou art the Son of God. (MARK 3:11)

19. And he ordained twelve, that they should be with him, and that he might send them forth to PREACH, and to have POWER to heal sicknesses, and to cast out devils. (MARK 3:14-15)

20. And he called them unto him, and said unto them in parables, how can SATAN CAST OUT SATAN? (MARK 3:23)

21. And if a house be divided against itself, that house CANNOT STAND. (MARK 3:25)

22. But he that shall blaspheme against the HOLY GHOST hath never forgiveness, but is in danger of ENTERNAL DAMNATION. (MARK 3:29)

23. For whosoever shall do the will of God, the same is my brother, and my sister, and MOTHER. (MARK 3:35)

24. Hearken, behold, there went out a SOWER TO SOW. (MARK 4:3)

25. And he said unto them, know ye not this parable? And how then will ye know all PARABLES. (MARK 4:4-8)

26. The sower soweth the WORD. (MARK 4:14)

27. But when it is sown, it growth up and becometh GREATER than all herbs, and shooteth out GREAT BRANCHES so that the fowls of the air may lodge under the SHADOW of it. (MARK 4:32)

28. And he arose, and rebuked the wind, and said unto the sea, PEACE, BE STILL, and the wind ceased, and there was a great calm.(MARK 4:39)

29. For he said unto him, come out of the man, thy unclean spirit and he asked him WHAT IS THY NAME? And he answered, saying, my name is LEGION: for we are many. (MARK 5:8-9)

30. And forthwith Jesus gave them leave, and the unclean spirits went out and ENTERED INTO THE SWINE: and the herd ran violently down a steep place into the sea, (they were about two thousand) and were CHOKED IN THE SEA. (MARK 5:13)

31. Howbeit Jesus suffered him not, but saith unto him, go home to thy friends, and tell them HOW GREAT THINGS THE LORD HATH DONE, FOR THEE, and hath had COMPASSION on thee. (MARK 5:19)

32. And Jesus went with him and much people followed him, and thronged him. And a certain woman which had an ISSUE OF BLOOD TWELVE years, and had suffered many things of many physicians, and HAD SPENT ALL THAT SHE HAD, and was nothing bettered, but rather grew worse. When she had heard of Jesus, came in the press behind, and touched his garment. For she said, IF I MAY TOUCH but his clothes, I shall be whole. And straightway the FOUNTAIN OF HER BLOOD WAS DRIED UP; and she felt in her body that she was HEALED of that plague. And Jesus immediately knowing in himself that virtue had gone out of him, turned him about in the press, and said, WHO TOUCHED MY CLOTHES? And his disciples said unto him, thou seest the multitude thronging thee and sayest thou, who touched me? And he looked round about to see her that had done this things, but the woman fearing and trembling, knowing what was done in her, CAME AND FELL DOWN BEFORE HIM, and told him all the truth. And he said unto her, daughter, THY FAITH HATH MADE THEE WHOLE; go in peace, and be whole of thy plague. (MARK 5:24-34)

33. And whosoever shall not receive you, nor hear you, when ye depart thence, SHAKE OFF THE DUST UNDER YOUR FEET FOR A TESTIMONY AGAINST THEM. Verily I say unto you, it shall be more tolerable for Sodom and Gomorrha in the of judgement, than for that city. (MARK 6:11)

34. But when Herod heard thereof, he said IT IS JOHN, WHOM I BEHEADED: he is risen from the dead. (MARK 6:16)

35. For John had said unto Herod, it is not lawful for thee to have THY BROTHER'S WIFE. (MARK 6:18)

36. And she went forth, and said unto her mother, what shall I ask? And she said, THE HEAD OF JOHN THE BAPTIST. (MARK 6:24)

37. And brought his head in a charger, and gave it to the damsel; and the damsel GAVE IT TO HER MOTHER. (MARK 6:28)

38. He saith unto them, how many loaves have ye? Go and see. And when they knew, they say, FIVE AND THREE FISHES. (MARK 6:38)

39. And they did all eat and were FILLED. (MARK 6:42)

40. And they that did eat of the loaves were about FIVE THOUSAND MEN. (MARK 6:44)

41. And when even was come, the ship was in the MIDST OF THE SEA, and he alone on the land. (MARK 6:47)

42. But when they saw him walking upon the sea, they supposed it had been A SPIRIT, and cried out: for they all saw him, and was troubled. AND IMMEDIATELY HE TALKED WITH THEM, and saith unto them, be of good cheer: IT IS I; be not afraid. (MARK 6:49-50)

43. There is nothing from without a man, that entering into him CAN DEFILE HIM; but the things which COME OUT OF HIM, those are they that defile the man. (MARK 7:15)

44. If any man have ears to hear, LET HIM HEAR. (MARK 7:16)

45. And were beyond measure astonished, saying, he hath done all things well: he MAKETH BOTH THE DEAF TO HEAR, AND THE DUMB TO SPEAK . (MARK 7:37)

46. And he sighed deeply in his spirit, and saith, why doth this generation seek after a sign? Verily I say unto you, there shall no sign be given UNTO THIS GENERATION. (MARK 8:12)

47. And he took the blind man by the hand, and led him out of town; and when he had spit on his eyes, and put his hands upon him, HE ASKED HIM IF HE SAW AUGHT and he looked up, and said I SEE MEN AS TREES, WALKING. After that he put his hands again upon his eyes and made him look up: and he was restored, AND SAW EVERY MAN CLEARLY. And he sent him away to his house, saying, neither go into the town, nor tell it to any in the town. (MARK 8:23-26)

48. And Jesus went out, and his disciples, into the towns of Caesarea Phillippi; and by the way he asked his disciples, saying unto them, Whom do men say that I am ? And they answered, JOHN THE BAPTIST; but some say, ELIAS; and others, ONE OF THE PROPHETS. And he saith unto them, But whom say ye that I am? And Peter answered and saith unto him, THOU ART THE CHRIST. (MARK 8:27-30)

49. And when he had called the people unto him with his disciples also, he said unto them, WHOSOEVER WILL COME AFTER ME, let him deny himself, AND TAKE UP HIS CROSS, AND FOLLOW ME. (MARK 8:34)

50. And after six days Jesus taketh with him Peter, and James and John and leadeth them up into an high mountain apart by themselves: and HE WAS TRANSFIGURED BEFORE THEM. And there appeared unto them ELIAS with MOSES and they were TALKING WITH JESUS. (MARK 9:2-4)

51. And as they came down from the mountain, he charged them they should tell no man what things they had seen, till the SON OF MAN WERE RISEN FROM THE DEAD. (MARK 9:9)

52. And one of the multitude answered and said, MASTER, I have brought unto thee my son, WHICH HATH A DUMB SPIRIT; and wheresoever he taketh him, HE TEARETH HIM; and he foamed, and gnasheth with his teeth, and pineth away; and I spake to thy disciples that they should cast him out; AND THEY COULD NOT. (MARK 9:17-18)

53. And he asked his father, How long is it ago since this came unto him? And he said, OF A CHILD. And oftimes it hath cast him into the FIRE, and into the WATER, to destroy him; but if thou canst do any thing, HAVE COMPASSION ON US AND HELP US. Jesus said unto him, if thou canst believe, ALL THINGS ARE POSSIBLE TO HIM THAT BELIEVE. And straightway the father of the child cried out, and said with tears, Lord, I believe; HELP THOU MINE UNBELIEF. When Jesus saw that the people came running together, he rebuked the foul spirit, saying unto him THOU DUMB AND DEAF SPIRIT, I charge thee, come out of him, and ENTER NO MORE INTO HIM. And the spirit cried, and rent him sore, and CAME OUT OF HIM and he was as one dead ; insomuch that many said, he is dead. But Jesus took him by the hand, and lifted him up and he arose. And when he was come into the house, his disciples asked him privately, Why COULD NOT we cast him out? And he

said unto them, this KIND can come forth by nothing, but by PRAYER AND FASTING. (MARK 9:21-29)

54. For he taught his disciples, and said unto them, the Son of man is delivered into the hands of men, and they shall kill him; and after that he is killed, he shall RISE THE THIRD DAY. But they UNDERSTOOD NOT that saying, and were afraid to ask him. (MARK 9:31-32)

55. But they held their peace; for by the way they had disputed among themselves, WHO SHOULD BE THE GREATEST. (MARK 9:34)

56. Whosoever shall receive one of such children in my name, RECEIVETHL ME and whosoever shall receive me, receiveth not me, BUT HIM THAT SENT ME. (MARK 9:37)

57. For he that is not against us IS ON OUR PART. (MARK 9:40)

58. Where their worm dieth NOT, and the fire is not QUENCHED. (MARK 9:44/46/48)

59. And the Pharisees came to him and asked him, is it lawful for a man to PUT AWAY his wife? Tempting him. And he answered and said unto them, what did MOSES COMMAND YOU? (MARK 10:2-3)

60. And he saith unto them, whosoever shall put away his wife and marry another, committeth ADULTERY AGAINST HER. And if a woman shall put away her husband, and be married to another, she committeth ADULTERY. (MARK 10:11-12)

61. But when Jesus saw it, he was much displeased, and said unto them, suffer the little children to come unto me, and FORBID THEM NOT; for of such is the kingdom of God. Verily I say unto you, whosoever shall not receive the kingdom of God as a little child, he shall not enter therein. And he took them up in his arms, put his hands upon them, and BLESSED THEM. (MARK 10:14-17)

62. It is easier for a camel to go through the eye of a needle, than for A RICH MAN to enter into the kingdom of God. (MARK 10:25)

63. And Jesus looking upon them saith, with men it is IMPOSSIBLE, but not with God: for with God ALL THINGS ARE POSSIBLE. (MARK 10:27)

64. They said unto him, GRANT UNTO US that we may sit, ONE on the thy right hand, and the OTHER on thy left hand, in thy glory. (MARK 10:37)

65. For even the Son of man came not to be ministered unto, but to minister, and to give his life A RANSOM FOR MANY. (MARK 10:45)

66. And Jesus said unto him, go thy way; THY FAITH HATH MADE THEE WHOLE. And immediately he received his sight, and followed Jesus in the way. (MARK 10:52)

67. And Peter calling to remembrance saith unto him, Master, behold, the fig tree which thou cursedst is withered away. And Jesus answering saith unto them, HAVE FAITH IN GOD. For verily I say unto you, that whosoever shall say unto this mountain, be thou removed, and be thou cast into the sea, and SHALL NOT DOUBT IN HIS HEART, but shall believe that those things which he saith shall come to pass; he SHALL HAVE WHATSOEVER HE SAITH. Therefore I say unto you, what things soever ye desire, when ye pray, BELIEVE that ye RECEIVE THEM, and ye shall have them. (MARK 11:21-24)

68. And he began to speak unto them in parables. A certain man PLANTED A VINEYARD, and set an hedge about it, and digged a place for the winevat, and built a tower, and let it out to husbandmen, and went into a far country. (MARK 12:1)

69. And Jesus answered him, The first of all the commandments is, Hear, O Israel; the Lord our God is one Lord: and thou shalt love the Lord thy God with all thy HEART, and with all they SOUL, and with all thy MIND, and with all thy STRENGTH; this is the first commandment. And the second is like, namely this, Thou shalt love thy NEIGHBOUR as thy thyself. There is none other commandment greater than these. (MARK 12:29-31)

70. And the gospel must first be published among ALL NATIONS. (MARK 13:10)

71. But when they shall lead you, and deliver you up, TAKE NO THOUGHT beforehand what ye shall speak, neither do ye premeditate: but whatsoever shall be given you in that hour, that speak ye; for it is not ye that speak, BUT THE HOLY GHOST. (MARK 13:11)

72. And then shall they see the Son of man coming in the clouds with great POWER AND GLORY. (MARK 13:26)

73. Heaven and earth shall pass away: but my words SHALL NOT PASS AWAY. (MARK 13:31)

74. But of that day and that hour knoweth no man, no, not the angels which are in heaven, neither the Son, BUT THE FATHER. (MARK 13;32)

75. And what I say unto you I say unto all, WATCH. (MARK 13:37)

76. And Jesus said, LET HER ALONE, why trouble ye her? She hath wrought a good work ON ME. (MARK 14:6)

77. And he sent forth two of his disciples and saith unto them, go ye into the city, and shall meet you a man bearing A PITCHER OF WATER; follow him. (MARK 14:13)

78. And he will show you a LARGE UPPER ROOM furnished and prepared: there make ready for us. (MARK 14:15)

79. And as they sat and did eat, Jesus said, verily I say unto you, one of you which eateth with me SHALL BETRAY ME. (MARK 14:18)

80. After the eating and drinking of the Last Supper, Jesus said unto them, this is my blood of the NEW TESTAMENT which is shed for many. (MARK 14:24)

81. And when they had sung a hymn, they went out into the MOUNT OF OLIVES. (MARK 14:26)

82. And Jesus saith unto him, verily I say unto thee, that this day, even in this night, before the cock crow twice, THOU SHALL DENY ME THRICE. (MARK 14:30)

83. Watch ye and pray, lest ye enter into temptation, the SPIRIT TRULY IS READY, but the flesh is weak. (MARK 14:38)

84. And he cometh the third time, and saith unto them, SLEEP ON NOW, and take your rest: it is enough, THE HOUR IS COME: behold, the Son of man is betrayed into the hands of sinners. (MARK 14:41)

85. And Jesus said, I AM; and ye shall see the Son of man sitting on the RIGHT HAND OF POWER and coming in the clouds of heaven. (MARK 14:62)

86. And they cried out again, CRUCIFY HIM. (MARK 15:13)

87. And they clothed him WITH PURPLE, AND PLAITED A crown of thorns. (MARK 15:17)

88. And they compel one Simon a Cyrenian, who passed by, coming out of the country, the father of Alexander and Rufus TO BEAR HIS CROSS. (MARK 15:21)

89. And they bring him unto the place Golgotha, which is being interpreted, THE PLACE OF THE SKULL. (MARK 15:22)

90. And they gave him to drink wine mingled with myrrh: but he received it NOT. (MARK 15:23)

91. And when they had crucified him, they parted his garments, CASTING LOTS UPON THEM, what every man should take. (MARK 15:24)

92. Likewise also the chief priests mocking said among themselves with the scribes, he saved others, HIMSELF HE CANNOT SAVE. (MARK 15:31)

93. And when the sixth hour was come, there was darkness over the whole land until the NINETH hour. (MARK 15:33)

94. And Jesus cried with a LOUD VOICE, and gave up the ghost. (MARK 15:37)

95. And he saith unto them, be not affrighted: ye seek Jesus of Nazareth, which was crucified: HE IS RISEN; HE IS NOT HERE: behold the place where they laid him. (MARK 16:6)

96. Now when Jesus was risen early the first day of the week, he appeared first to MARY MAGDALENE, out of whom he had cast SEVEN DEVILS. (MARK 16:9)

97. Afterward he appeared unto THE ELEVEN as they sat at meat, and upbraided them with their unbelief and hardness of heart, because they believed NOT THEM, WHICH HAD SEEN HIM AFTER HE WAS RISEN. (MARK 16:14)

98. And he said unto them: go ye into all the world, and PREACH THE GOSPEL TO EVERY CREATURE. He that BELIEVETH and is BAPTIZED shall be saved; but he that believeth not shall be damned. And these signs shall FOLLOW THEM THAT BELIEVE; in my name shall they CAST OUT DEVILS; they shall speak with NEW TONGUES. They shall TAKE UP SERPENTS; and if they drink any DEADLY THING, it shall not hurt them; they shall LAY HAND ON THE SICK, and they shall recover. So then after the Lord had spoken unto them, he was RECEIVED UP INTO HEAREN and SAT ON THE RIGHT HAND OF GOD. And they went forth, and preached every where, the Lord working with them and CONFIRMING THE WORD WITH SIGNS FOLLOWING. (MARK 16:15-20)

THE END ST. MARK

ST. LUKE

1. And they were both righteous before God, walking in all the commandments and ordinances of the Lord, BLAMELESS. And they had no child, because that Elisabeth WAS BARREN, and they both were now well stricken in years. (LUKE 1:6-7)

2. And there appeared unto him an angel of the Lord standing on the right side of the altar of incense. But the angel said unto him fear not Zacharias; for thy prayer is heard; and thy wife Elisabeth SHALL BEAR THEE A SON, and thou shalt call his name JOHN. (LUKE 1:11-13

3. And Zacharias said unto the angel, whereby shall I know this? For I am an old man and my wife well stricken in years. And the angel answering said unto him, I AM GABRIEL, THAT STAND IN THE PRESENT OF GOD and am sent to speak unto thee, and to show thee these glad tidings. And behold, THEY SHALL BE DUMB AND NOT ABLE TO SPEAK, until the day that these things shall be performed, because thou BELIEVEST NOT my words, which shall be fulfilled in their season. And when he came out he could not speak unto them and they perceived that he had seen a vision in the temple, for he beckoned unto them, and REMAINED SPEECHLESS. (LUKE 1:18-20)

4. And in the sixth month THE ANGEL GABRIEL was sent from God unto a city of Galilee, named Nazareth. (LUKE 1:26)

5. And the angel said unto her, fear not Mary; for thou hast found FAVOUR WITH GOD. (LUKE 1:30)

6. And, behold, thou shall conceive in thy womb, and bring forth a son, and shall call his name JESUS. (LUKE 1:31)

7. Then said Mary unto the angel, how shall this be, SEEING I KNOW NOT A MAN? (LUKE 1:34)

8. And the angel answered and said unto her the Holy Ghost shall come upon thee, and the POWER OF THE HIGHEST shall overshadow thee; therefore also that holy thing which shall be born of thee shall be called THE SON OF MAN. And behold, thy cousin ELISABETH, she hath also conceived a son in HER OLD AGE; and this is the sixth month with her, WHO WAS BARREN. For with God NOTHING SHALL BE IMPOSSIBLE. (LUKE 1:35-37)

9. And Mary said, behold the handmaid of the Lord; be it unto me ACCORDING TO THY WORD. (LUKE 1:38)

10. And Mary said, my soul doth MAGNIFY the Lord. (LUKE 1:14)

11. Now Elisabeth's full time came that she should be delivered; and she brought forth A SON. (LUKE 1:57)

12. And he asked for a writing table, and wrote, saying HIS NAME IS JOHN. (LUKE 1:63)

13. And his mouth was opened immediately, and his tongue loosed and HE SPAKE AND PRAISED GOD. (LUKE 1:64)

14. And the child grew, and waxed strong in spirit, and was in the deserts till the day his SHOWING UNTO ISRAEL. (LUKE 1;80)

15. And she brought forth her firstborn son, and wrapped him in SWADDLING CLOTHES, and laid him in a manger; because there was no room for them in the inn. (LUKE 2:7)

16. Glory to God in the hightest, and on earth peace, GOOD WILL TOWARD MEN (LUKE 2:14)

17. And when eight days were accomplished for the CIRCUMCISING OF THE CHILD, his name was called JESUS, which was so named of the angel before he was CONCEIVED IN THE WOMB. (LUKE 2:21

18. And behold, there was a man in Jerusalem, whose name was Simeon; and the same man was just and devout, waiting for the consolation of Israel; AND THE HOLY GHOST WAS UPON HIM. And it was revealed unto him by the Holy Ghost, that he should not SEE DEATH, before he had seen the Lord's Christ. And he CAME BY THE SPIRIT into the temple; and when the parents brought in the child Jesus, to do for him after the custom of the law, Then took he him up in his arms, and BLESSED GOD, and said, Lord, now lettest thou thy SERVANT DEPART IN PEACE. according to thy word. For mine eyes have seen thy SALVATION. (LUKE2:29)

19. Now his parent went to Jerusalem every year at the feast of the Passover, and when he was TWELVE YEARS OLD, they went up to Jerusalem after the custom of the feast. (LUKE2:41-42)

20. And when they had fulfilled the days, as they returned, the child TARRIED BEHIND in Jerusalem and Joseph and his mother KNEW NOT OF IT. (LUKE 2:43)

21. And it came to pass, that after three days they found him in the temple, SITTING IN THE MIDST OF THE DOCTORS, both hearing them, and asking them questions. (LUKE 2:46)

22. And he said unto them, How is it that ye sought me? Wist ye not that I MUST BE ABOUT MY FATHER'S BUSINESS. (LUKE 2:49)

23. And Jesus increased in wisdom and stature, and in FAVOUR WITH GOD AND MAN. (LUKE 2:52)

24. Every valley shall be filled, and every mountain and hill shall be brought low; and the crooked shall be made straight, and the rough ways shall be made smooth; and all flesh SHALL SEE THE SALVATION OF GOD. (LUKE 3:2-3)

25. Then said he to the multitude that came forth to be BAPTIZED OF HIM, O generation of vipers, who hath warned you to flee from THE WRATH TO COME? (LUKE 3:5-6)

26. John answered, saying unto them all, I indeed baptize you with water; BUT ONE MIGHTIER THAN I COMETH, the latchet of whose shoes I am not worthy to unloose; he shall baptize you with THE HOLY GHOST AND WITH FIRE. (LUKE 3:16)

27. Added yet this above all, that he shut up JOHN IN PRISON. (LUKE 3:20)

28. Now when all the people were baptized, it came to pass, that Jesus also being baptized, and praying, the heaven was opened, and the Holy Ghost descended in a bodily shape like a dove upon him, and A VOICE CAME FROM HEAVEN, which said, Thou art my beloved Son, IN THEE I AM WELL PLEASED. (LUKE 3:21-22)

29. And Jesus himself began to be about THIRTY YEARS OF AGE. (LUKE 3:23)

30. And Jesus being full of THE HOLY GHOST returned from Jordan, and was led by the spirit into the wilderness, being FORTY DAYS tempted by the devil. And in those days he did EAT NOTHING: and when they were ended, he afterward hungered. (LUKE 4:1-2)

31. And when the devil had ended all the temptations, HE DEPARTED FROM HIM FOR A SEASON. (LUKE 4:13)

32. And he came to Nazareth, where he had been brought up: and as his custom was, he went into the synagogue ON THE SABBATH DAY and stood up to read. And there was delivered unto him THE BOOK OF THE PROPHET ESAIAS. And when he had opened the book, he found the place where it was written: THE SPIRIT OF THE LORD IS UPON ME, because he hath anointed me to preach the gospel to the poor, he hath sent me to heal the brokenhearted, to preach deliverance to the captives and recovering of sight to the blind, to set at liberty them that are bruised, to preach, the acceptable year of the Lord. And he closed the book, and gave it back to the minister, and sat down. And the EYES OF ALL THEM THAT WERE IN THE SYNAGOGUE were fastened on him. And he began to say unto them, this day is this scripture FULFILLED IN YOUR EARS. (LUKE 4:16-21)

33. And they were astonished at his doctrine FOR HIS WORD WAS WITH POWER. (LUKE 4:32)

34. And they were all amazed, and spake among themselves, saying, what a word is this! For with AUTHORITY AND POWER he commandeth the unclean spirits, and they come out. (LUKE 4:36)

35. And devils also came out of many, crying out, and saying, Thou art Christ the Son of God. And he rebuking them suffered them not to speak: FOR THEY KNEW THAT HE WAS CHRIST. (LUKE 4:41)

36. And Simon answering said unto him, Master, WE HAVE TOILED ALL THE NIGHT, AND HAVE TAKEN NOTHING: nevertheless at thy word I will let down the net. And when they had this done, they inclosed A GREAT MULTITUDE OF FISHES; and their net brake. (LUKE 5:5-6)

37. And it came to pass on a certain day, as he was teaching, that there were PHARISEES AND DOCTORS OF THE LAW SITTING BY, which were come out of every town of Galilee, and Judaea, and Jerusalem: and the power of the Lord WAS PRESENT TO HEAL THEM. (LUKE 5:17)

38. And they that were vexed with unclean spirits; and THEY WERE HEALED the whole multitude SOUGHT TO TOUCH HIM for there went virtue out of him, and healed them all. (LUKE 6:18-19)

39. But I say unto you which hear, Love your enemies, DO GOOD TO THEM WHICH HATE YOU. Bless them that curse you, and PRAY FOR THEM which despitefully use you. (LUKE 6:27-28)

40. But love ye your enemies, and do good, and lend, hoping for nothing again AND YOUR REWARD SHALL BE GREAT and ye shall be the children of the Highest: for he is kind unto the unthankful and to the evil. (LUKE 6:35)

41. Judge not, and ye shall not be judged. Condemn not and ye shall not be condemned; forgive, AND YE SHALL BE FORGIVEN. (LUKE 6:37)

42. And why call ye me, Lord, Lord, and do not the things which I say? Whosoever cometh to me, AND HEARETH MY SAYINGS, AND DOETH THEM, I will show you to whom he is like: He is like a man which built an house and digged deep, and laid the foundation on a rock and when the flood arose, the stream beat vehemently upon that house, AND COULD NOT SHAKE IT; for it was found upon a rock. (LUKE 6:46-48)

43. And when the Lord saw her, he had COMPASSION on her, and said unto her, weep not. (LUKE 7:13)

44. For I say unto you, among those that are born of women there is not a breater prophet than JOHN THE BAPTIST; but he that is least in the kingdom of God is greater than he. (LUKE 7:28)

45. And, behold, a woman in the city, which was a sinner, when she knew that Jesus sat at meat in the Pharisee's house, brought an alabaster box of ointment, and stood at his feet behind him weeping, AND BEGAN TO WASH HIS FEET WITH TEARS, and did wipe them with the hairs of her head, and kissed his feet, and anointed them with the ointment. (LUKE 7:37-38)

46. And he said unto her, thy sins are FORGIVEN. (LUKE 7:48)

47. And he said to the woman THY FAITH hath saved thee; go in peace. (LUKE 7:50)

48. Now the parable is this: the seed is the word of GOD. (LUKE 8:11)

49. And Jesus said, somebody hath touched me: for I perceive that VIRTUE IS GONE OUT OF ME. (LUKE 8:46)

50. But when Jesus heard it, he answered him saying, fear not BELIEVE ONLY, and she shall be made whole. (LUKE 8:50)

51. Then he called his twelve disciples together, and gave them POWER AND AUTHORITY over all devils, and to cure diseases. (LUKE 9:1)

52. And whosoever will not receive you, when ye go out of that city, shake off the very dust from your feet FOR A TESTIMONY AGAINST THEM. (LUKE 9:5)

53. For they were about five thousand men. And he said to his disciples make them sit down by FIFTIES IN A COMPANY. (LUKE 9:14)

54. And it came to pass, as he was alone praying, his disciples were with him; and he asked them, saying, Whom say the people that I am? They answering said, John the Baptist; but some say, Elias; and others say, that one of the old prophets is risen again. He said unto them, BUT WHOM SAY YE THAT I AM? Peter answering said, The Christ of God. (LUKE 9:18-20)

55. And he straitly charged them, and commanded them to tell NO MAN THAT THING. (LUKE 9:21)

56. And behold, there talked with him two men, which were MOSES AND ELIAS. (LUKE 9:30)

57. While he thus spake, there came a cloud, and overshadowed them and they feared as they entered into the cloud. And there came a voice out of the cloud, saying, This is my beloved Son: HEAR HIM. (LUKE 9:34-35

58. And Jesus said unto him, forbid him not; for he that is NOT AGAINST US IS FOR US. (LUKE 9:50)

59. And Jesus said unto him, foxes have holes, and birds of the air have nests but the Son of man hath NO WHERE TO LAY HIS HEAD. (LUKE 9:58)

60. After these things the Lord appointed other SEVENTY also, and sent them two and two before his face into every city and place, whither he himself would come. And unto the mission of the SEVENTY he said; the harvest truly is great BUT THE LABORERS ARE FEW; pray ye therefore the Lord of the harvest, that he would send forth laborers into his harvest. Go your ways; behold, I SEND YOU FORTH AS LAMBS AMONG WOLVES. (LUKE 10:1-3)

61. And the seventy returned again with joy, saying, Lord even the devils are subject unto us THROUGH THY NAME. And he said unto them I beheld Satan as lighting fall from heaven. Behold, I give unto you POWER to tread on serpents and scorpions, and over all the POWER OF THE ENEMY and nothing shall by any means hurt you. Notwithstanding in this rejoice not, that the spirits are subject unto you; but rather rejoice, because YOUR NAMES ARE WRITTEN IN HEAVEN. (LUKE 10:17-20)

62. And behold, a certain lawyer stood up, and tempted him, saying, Master, WHAT SHALL I DO TO INHERIT ETERNAL LIFE? He said unto him, what is written in the law? How readest thou? LUKE 10:25-26)

63. Which now of these three, thinkest thou, was neighbour unto him that FELL AMONG THE THIEVES? And he said, he that showed mercy on him. Then Jesus said unto him GO AND DO THOU LIKEWISE. (LUKE 10:36-37)

64. But one thing is needful; and Mary HAS CHOSEN THAT GOOD PART, which shall not be taken away from her. (LUKE 10:42)

65. And it came to pass, that, as he was praying in a certain place, when he ceased, one of his disciples said unto him, LORD TEACH US TO PRAY, as John also taught his disciples. (LUKE 11:1)

66. And I say unto you ASK, and it shall be given you SEEK, and ye shall find KNOCK, and it shall be opened unto you. For every one that ASKETH receiveth, and he that SEEKETH findeth, and to him that KNOCKETH it shall be opened.(LUKE 11:9-10)

67. He that is not with me is AGAINST me; and he that gathered not with me SCATTERED. (LUKE 11:23)

68. And as he spake, a certain Pharisee besougth him to dine with him; and he went in and SAT DOWN TO MEAT, and when the Pharisee saw it, he marveled that he had not FIRST WASHED BEFORE DINNER. And the Lord said unto him; now do ye Pharisees make clean the outside of the cup and the platter but your INWARD PART is full of RAVENING AND WICKEDNESS. (LUKE 11:37-39)

69. For there is nothing covered, that shall not BE REVEALED; neither hid, that shall not BE KNOWN. (LUKE 12:2)

70. And whosoever shall speak a word against the Son of man it shall be FORGIVEN HIM. But unto him that BLASPHEMETH against the HOLY GHOST it shall not be forgiven. (LUKE 12:10)

71. And when they bring you into the synagogues, and unto magistrates and powers, take ye no thought how or what thing ye shall answer or what ye SHALL SAY; For the HOLY GHOST SHALL TEACH YOU in the same hour what ye ought to say. (LUKE 12:11-12)

72. But rather seek ye the kingdom of God and all these things shall BE ADDED UNTO YOU. (LUKE 12:31)

73. Be ye therefore ready also; for the Son of man cometh at an hour WHEN YE THINK NOT. (LUKE 12:40)

74. And that servant, which knew his lord's will, and prepared not himself, neither did according to his will, shall be BEATEN WITH MANY STRIPES. (LUKE 12:47)

75. And, behold, there was a woman which had A SPIRIT OF INFIRMITY eighteen years and was bowed together, and could in no wise LIFT UP HERSELF. And Jesus saw her, he called her to him, and said unto her WOMAN, THOU ARE LOOSED FROM THINE INFIRMITY, and he laid his hands on her and immediately she was made straight and GLORIFIED GOD. (LUKE 13:11-13)

76. And ought not this woman, being a daughter of Abraham, WHOM SATAN HATH BOUND, lo thou eighteen years, be loosed from this bond on the Sabbath day? (LUKE 13:16)

77. There shall be weeping and gnashing of teeth, when ye shall see ABRAHAM AND ISAAC AND JACOB, and all prophets, in the kingdom of God, and you yourselves thrust out. (LUKE 13:28)

78. And, behold, there are last which shall be first, and there are FIRST WHICH SHALL BE LAST. (LUKE 13:30)

79. But when thou makest a feast, call the poor, the maimed, the lame, the blind, and thou shall be BLESSED; for they cannot recompense thee; for thou shall be RECOMPENSE AT THE RESURRECTION OF THE JUST. (LUKE 14:13-14)

80. I say unto you, that likewise joy shall be in heaven over one SINNER THAT REPENTETH, more than over ninety and nine just persons, which need NO REPENTANCE. (LUKE 15:7)

81. Likewise, I say unto you, there is joy in the present of the ANGELS OF GOD over one sinner that repenteth. (LUKE 15:10)

82. It was meet that we should make merry, and be glad; for this thy brother was DEAD and is alive again; and WAS LOST AND IS FOUND. (LUKE 15:32)

83. There was a certain rich man, which was clothed in PURPLE AND FINE LINEN, and fared sumptuously EVERY DAY. And there was a certain begger named LAZARUS, which was laid at his gate, full of sores, and desiring to be fed with the CRUMBS which fell from the rich man's table; moreover the dogs came and licked his sores. And it came to pass, the begger died, and was CARRIED BY THE ANGELS INTO ABRAHAM'S BOSOM: the rich man also died, and was buried; AND IN HELL HE LIFTED UP HIS EYES, being in torments, and seeth Abraham afar off, and Lazarus in his bosom. And he cried and said Father Abraham have mercy on me, and send Lazarus, that he may DIP THE TIP OF HIS FINGER IN WATER and cool my tongue, for I am tormented in this flame. (LUKE 16:19-24)

84. And he said unto him, if they hear not MOSES AND THE PROPHETS neither will they be persuaded, though one rose from the dead. (LUKE 16:31

85. Take heed to yourselves; if thy brother trespass against thee, rebuke him! And if he repent, FORGIVE HIM. (LUKE 17:3)

86. And as he entered into a certain village, there met him TEN MEN that were lepers, which stood afar off. (LUKE 17:12)

87. And when he saw them, he said unto them, go show yourselves unto the priest, and it cam to pass, that, as they went, THEY WERE CLEANED. (LUKE 17:14)

88. And one of them, when he saw that he was healed, TURNED BACK and with a loud voice GLORIFIED GOD. (LUKE 17:15)

89. And Jesus answering said were there not ten cleaned? BUT WHERE ARE THE OTHER NINE? (LUKE 17:17)

90. And he said unto him, arise, go thy way; thy FAITH hath made thee whole. (LUKE 17:19)

91. Neither shall they say, lo here! Or lo there! For behold, the kingdom of God IS WITHIN YOU. (LUKE 17:21)

92. Remember Lot's WIFE. (LUKE 17:32)

93. And he said, the things which are impossible with men ARE POSSIBLE WITH GOD. (LUKE 18:27)

94. And Jesus said unto him, receive thy sight THY FAITH HATH SAVED THEE. (LUKE 18:42).

95. And immediately he received his sight, and followed him, GLORIFYING GOD and all the people, when they saw it, gave praise unto God. (LUKE 18:43)

96. And Jesus said unto him, This day is salvation come to this house, forasmuch as he also is A SON OF ABRAHAM. For the Son of man is come to seek and to save . (LUKE 19:9-10)

97. And when he had thus spoken, he went before ASCENDING UP TO JERUSALEM. (LUKE 19:28)

98. Saying, Blessed be the king that cometh in the name of the Lord, PEACE IN HEAVEN, AND GLORY IN THE HIGHTEST. (LUKE 19:38)

99. And some of the Pharisees from among the multitude said unto him, Master, REBUKE THY DISCIPLES. (LUKE 19:39)

100. And he answered and said unto them, I tell you that, if these should hold their peace, THE STONE WOULD IMMEDIATELY CRY OUT. (LUKE 19:40)

101. Show me a penny. Whose image and superscription hath it? They answered and said CAESAR'S. And he said unto them, RENDER THEREFORE UNTO CAESAR the things which be Caesar's, and unto GOD THE THINGS WHICH BE GOD. (LUKE 20:25)

102. And the third took her; and in like manner the seven also: and they left no children and died. Last of all the woman died also. Therefore in the resurrection, WHOSE WIFE OF THEM IS SHE? For seven had her to wife. And Jesus answering said unto them, the children OF THIS WORLD MARRY, and are given in marriage. But they which shall be accounted worthy to obtain that world, and the resurrection from the dead, NEITHER MARRY, NOR ARE GIVEN IN MARRIAGE. (LUKE 20:31-35)

103. Heaven and earth shall pass away, but MY WORD SHALL NOT pass away. (LUKE 21:33)

104. Watch ye therefore, and PRAY ALWAYS, that ye may be ACCOUNTED WORTHY to escape all these things that shall come to pass, and to stand before the Son of man. (LUKE 21:36)

105. Now the feast of unleavened bread drew nigh, which is called THE PASSOVER. And the chief priest and scribes sought how they might kill him; for they feared the people. Then entered SATAN into Judas surnamed ISCARIOT being of the number of the TWELVE. And he went his way and communed with the chief priest and captain, how he might betray him unto them. And they were glad, and COVENANT to give him money. And he promised and sought opportunity to betray him unto them on the absent of the multitude. Then came the day of unleavened bread, when the Passover must be killed. And he sent PETER AND JOHN saying, go and prepare us the Passover, that we may eat. And they said unto him, where wilt thou that we prepare? And he said unto them, behold, when ye are entered into the city, THERE SHALL A MAN MEET YOU, bearing a pitcher of water, follow him into the house where he entereth in. and ye shall say unto the Goodman of the house, the Master saith

unto thee, WHERE IS THE GUESTCHAMBER, where I shall eat the Passover with my disciples? And he shall show you a large upper room FURNISHED: there make ready.(LUKE 22:1-12)

106. And he took the cup, and gave thanks, and said, take this, and divide it among yourselves. For I say unto you, I WILL NOT DRINK OF THE FRUIT OF THE VINE, until the kingdom of God shall come. And he took bread, and gave thanks, and brake it, and gave unto them saying THIS IS MY BODY which is given for you; THIS DO IN REMEMBRANCE OF ME. Likewise also the cup after supper, saying, this cup is the NEW TESTAMENT IN MY BLOOD, which is shed for you. (LUKE 22:17-20))

107. And the Lord said,k Simon, Simon, behold, Satan hath desired to have you, that he may sift you as wheat. But I have prayed for thee, that THY FAITH FAIL NOT and when thou art converted, strengthen thy brethren. (LUKE 22:31-32)

108. And he said unto them, when I sent you without purse, and scrip, and shoes, lacked ye anything? And they said NOTHING. (LUKE 22:35)

109. And when he was at the place, he said unto them pray that ye enter not INTO TEMPTATION. (LUKE 22:40)

110. And while he ye spake, behold a multitude, and he that was called Judas, one of th twelve, went before them, and drew near unto Jesus to KISS HIS. But Jesus said unto him, Judas betrayest thou the Son of man   WITH A KISS? (LUKE 22:47-48)

111. And one of them smote the servant of the high priest and CUT OFF HIS RIGHT EAR. And Jesus answered and said suffer ye thus far. And he touched his ear, AND HEALED HIM. (LUKE 22:50-51)

112. And the Lord turned, and looked upon Peter, and Peter remembered the word of the Lord, how he had said unto him, before the cock crow; thou shall deny me thrice. And Peter went out, and WEPT BITTERLY. (LUKE 22:61-62)

113. And the whole multitude of them arose, and led him unto PILATE. (LUKE 23:1)

114. Then he questioned with him in many words; BUT HE ANSWERED HIM NOTHING. (LUKE 23:9)

115. And the same day, Pilate and Herod were made FRIENDS TOGETHER for before they were at enmity between themselves. (LUKE 23:12)

116. I will therefore chastise him, and RELEASE HIM. (LUKE 23:16)

117. But they cried, saying, crucify him, CRUCIFY HIM. (LUKE 23:21)

118. Then said Jesus, Father, forgive them; for they know not what they do. And they PARTED HIS RAIMENT AND CAS LOTS. (LUKE 23:34)

119. And he said unto Jesus, Lord remember me when thou comest into thy kingdom.   And Jesus said unto him, verily I say unto thee, TODAY SHALT THOU BE WITH ME IN PARADISE. (LUKE 23:42-43)

120. And when Jesus had cried with a loud voice, he said FATHER, INTO THY HANDS I COMMEND MY SPIRIT: and having said thus, he gave up the ghost. (LUKE 23:46)

121. This man went unto Pilate, and begged the body of JESUS and he took it down, and WRAPPED IT IN LINEN, and laid it in a sepulchre that was hewn in stone, wherein NEVER man before was laid.(LUKE 23:52-53

122. And they returned, and prepared spices and ointments and RESTED THE SABBATH DAY ACCORDING TO THE COMMANDMENT. (LUKE 23:56)

123. And they found the stone ROLLED AWAY from the sepulchre. (LUKE 24:2)

124. And they entered in and found NOT the body of the Lord Jesus. (LUKE 24:3)

125. And it came to pass, as they were much perplexed thereabout, behold, two men stood by them in SHINING GARMENTS. (LUKE 24:4)

126. He is not here, but is risen; remember how he spake unto you when he was yet in Galilee saying, the Son of man must be delivered into the hands of sinful men, and be crucified, AND THE THIRD DAY RISE AGAIN. (LUKE 24:6-7)

127. And they remembered his WORDS. (LUKE 24:8)

128. Then arose Peter, and ran unto the sepulchre; and stooping down, he beheld the LINEN CLOTHES LAID BY THEMSELVES, and departed, wondering in himself at that which was COME TO PASS. (LUKE 24:12)

129. And he said unto them, what things? And they said unto him, concerning JESUS OF NAZARETH, which was a prophet mighty in deed and word before God and all the people. (LUKE 24:19)

130. And when they found not his body, they came, saying that they had also SEEN A VISION OF ANGELS, which said that he was ALIVE. (LUKE 24:23)

131. But they constrained him, saying, abide with us; for it is toward evening, and the day is far spent. And he went in TO TARRY WITH THEM. (LUKE 24:29)

132. And their eyes were opened AND THEY KNEW HIM; and he vanished out of their sight. (LUKE 24:31)

133. And he said unto them, why are ye troubled? And why do THOUGHTS ARISE IS YOUR HEARTS? (LUKE 24:38)

134. Behold, my hands and my feet, that it is I myself; handle me, and see; for a SPIRIT HATH NOT FLESH AND BONES, as ye see me have. (LUKE 24:39)

135. And when he had thus spoke, he showed them HIS HANDS AND HIS FEET. (LUKE 24:40)

136. Then opened he their understanding, that they might UNDERSTAND THE SCRIPTURES. (LUKE 24:45)

137. And that repentance and remission of sins should be preached in his name among all nations, BEGINNING AT JERUSALEM. And ye are WITNESS of these things. And behold, I send the promise of my Father upon you; but tarry ye in the city of JERUSALEM, UNTIL YE BE ENDUED WITH POWER FROM ON HIGH. And he let them out as far as to BETHANY, and he lifted up his hands AND BLESSED THEM.   And it came to pass, while he blessed them, he was parted from them and CARRIED UP INTO HEAVEN. And they worshipped him, and returned to JEURSALEM with great joy. And were continually in the temple, PRAISING AND BLESSING GOD. AMEN. (LUKE 24:47-53)

THE END ST. LUKE

ST. JOHN

1. In the beginning was the WORD and the WORD was with God, and the WORD was God. (ST. JOHN 1:1)

2. All things were made by HIM; and without HIM was not any thing made THAT WAS MADE. (ST. JOHN 1:3)

3. In him was LIFE and the LIFE was the LIGHT OF MEN. (ST. JOHN 1:4)

4. There was a man sent from GOD whose name was JOHN. (ST. JOHN 1:6)

5. The same came for a witness, TO BEAR WITNESS of the Light, that all men through him might believe. (ST. JOHN 1:7)

6. He was not that Light, but was sent to bear witness OF THAT LIGHT. (ST. JOHN 1:8)

7. Which were born, not of blood, nor of the will of the flesh, nor of the will of man, BUT OF GOD. (ST. JOHN 1:13)

8. John bare witness of him, and cried, saying, this was he of whom I spake, he that cometh after me is preferred before me: FOR HE WAS BEFORE ME. (ST. JOHN 1:15)

9. And John bare record, saying, I saw the SPIRIT DESCENDING FROM HEAVEN like a dove, and it abode upon him. (ST. JOHN 1:32)

10. And I saw, and bare record that this IS THE SON OF GOD. (ST. JOHN 1:34)

11. And he saith unto him, verily, verily, I say unto you, hereafter ye shall ye shall SEE HEAVEN OPEN, and the angels of God ASCENDING AND DESCENDING upon the Son of man. (ST. JOHN 1:51)

12. And both Jesus was called, and his disciples, to the MARRIAGE (ST. JOHN 2:2)

13. And when they wanted wine, the mother of Jesus saith unto him, THEY HAVE NO WINE. (ST. JOHN 2:3)

14. Jesus saith unto her, Woman, what have I to do with thee? MINE HOUR IS NOT YET COME. His mother saith unto the servants, whatsoever he saith unto you, DO IT. (ST. JOHN 2:4-5)

15. When the ruler of the feast had tasted the water, THAT WAS MADE WINE, and knew not whence it was (but the servants which drew the water knew) the governor of the feast called the BRIDEGROOM. (ST. JOHN 2:9)

16. This beginning of miracles did Jesus in Cana of Galilee, and manifested forth his glory; and his DISCIPLES BELIEVED ON HIM. (ST. JOHN 2:11)

17. Jesus answered and said unto them, destroy this temple, and IN THREE DAYS, I will raise it up. (ST. JOHN 2:19)

18. But he spake of the temple of his BODY. (ST. JOHN 2:21)

19. But Jesus did not commit himself unto them, because he knew ALL MEN. And needed not that any should testify of man: FOR HE KNEW WHAT WAS IN MAN (ST. JOHN 2:24-25)

20. Nicodemus saith unto him, How can a man be born when he is old? Can he enter the second time into his mother's womb and be born? Jesus answered, verily, verily, I say unto thee, except a man be BORN OF WATER AND OF THE SPIRIT HE CANNOT   enter into the kingdom of God. That which is born of the FLESH IS FLESH; and that which is born of the SPIRIT IS SPIRIT. Marvel not that I said unto thee, YE MUST BE BORN AGAIN. (ST. JOHN 3:4-7)

21. For God so loved the world, that he gave his only begotten Son, that whosoever BELIEVETH IN HIM should not perish, but have everlasting life.   (ST. JOHN 3:16)

22. And this is the condemnation, that light is come into the world, and men loved DARKNESS rather than LIGHT, because their deeds were evil.   For every one that doeth evil HATETH THE LIGHT, neither cometh to the light, lest his deeds should be reproved. But he that doeth truth COMETH TO THE LIGHT, that his deeds may be made manifest, that they are wrought in God. (ST. JOHN 3:19-21)

23. John answered and said, a man can receive nothing except it be given him from heaven. Ye yourselves bear me witness, that I said, I am not the Christ, BUT THAT I AM SENT BEFORE HIM. (ST. JOHN 3:27-28)

24. He that believeth on the Son hath everlasting life: and he that believeth not the Son shall not see life; BUT THE WRATH OF GOD ABIDETH ON HIM. (ST. JOHN 3:36)

25. Now Jacob's well was there, Jesus therefore, being wearied with his journey, SAT THUS ON THE WELL and it was about the sixth hour. There cometh a woman of Samaria to draw water: Jesus said unto her, GIVE ME TO DRINK. (ST. JOHN 4:6-7)

26. Jesus answered and said unto her: whosoever drinketh of this water SHALL THIRST AGAIN. But whosoever drinketh of the water that I shall give him SHALL NEVER THIRST; but the water that I give him shall be in him a well of water SPRINGING UP INTO EVERLASTING LIFE. (ST. JOHN 4:13-14)

27. The woman saith unto him, Sir, I perceive that thou art A PROPHET. (ST. JOHN 4:19)

28. God is a Spirit: and they that worship him MUST WORSHIP HIM IN SPIRIT AND IN TRUTH. (ST. JOHN 4:24)

29. Jesus saith unto her, I that speak unto thee AM HE. (ST. JOHN 4:26)

30. And said unto the woman now we believe, not because of thy saying: for we have heard him ourselves, and know that this is indeed the Christ, THE SAVIOR OF THE WORLD. (ST. JOHN 4:42)

31. Then said Jesus unto him, except ye see signs and wonders, ye will NOT BELIEVE (ST. JOHN 4:48)

32. The nobleman saith unto him, Sir, come down ere my child die. Jesus saith unto him, GO THY WAY, THY SON LIVETH. And the man BELIEVED the word that Jesus had spoken unto him, and went his way. And as he was now going down, his servants met him, and told him, saying, THY SON LIVETH. Then inquired he of them the HOUR WHEN HE BEGAN TO AMEND. And they said unto him, yesterday at the ELEVENTH HOUR the fever left him. So the father knew that it was at the SAME HOUR, in which Jesus said unto him

THY SON LIVETH and himself believed, and his whole house. This is again the SECOND MIRACLE that Jesus did, when he was come out of Judaea into Galilee. (ST. JOHN 4:49-54)

33. For an angel went down at a certain season into the pool, and TROUBLED THE WATER; whosoever then first after the troubling of the water stepped in was made whole of whatsoever disease he had. And a certain man was there, which had an infirmity THIRTY AND EIGHT YEARS. When Jesus saw him lie, and knew that he had been now a long time in that case, he saith unto him, WILT THOU BE MADE WHOLE? The impotent man answered him, Sir, I have no man, WHEN THE WATER IS TROUBLED, put me into the pool: but while I am coming, another steppeth down before me. Jesus saith unto him, RISE TAKE UP THY BED AND WALK. And immediately the man was made whole, and took up his bed, and walked: and on the same day was THE SABBATH. (ST. JOHN 5:4-9)

34. Afterward Jesus findeth him in the temple, and said unto him, behold, thou art made whole: SIN NO MORE, LEST A WORST THING COME UNTO THEE. (ST. JOHN 5:14)

35. For the Father judgeth no man, but hath committed ALL JUDGEMENT UNTO THE SON. (ST. JOHN 5:22)

36. Verily, verily, I say unto you he that heareth my word and BELIEVETH ON HIM THAT SENT ME has everlasting life, and shall not come into condemnation, but is passed from DEATH UNTO LIFE. (ST. JOHN 5:24)

37. And hath given him authority to execute judgement also, because he is the SON OF MAN. (ST. JOHN 5:27)

38. Ye sent unto John, and he BARE WITNESS unto the truth. (ST. JOHN 5:33)

39. For had ye believed Moses ye would have believed me FOR HE WROTE OF ME. (ST. JOHN 5:46)

40. There is a lad here, which hath five barley loaves and two small fishes: but what are they AMONG SO MANY? (ST. JOHN 6:9)

41. Therefore they gathered them together and filled twelve baskets with the fragment of five barley loaves, which remained OVER AND ABOVE unto them that had eaten. (ST. JOHN 6:13)

42. So when they had rowed about five and twenty or thirty furlong, they see Jesus WALKING ON LTHE SEA, and drawing nigh unto the ship: and they were afraid. But he saith unto them, it is I, BE NOT AFRAID. (ST. JOHN 6:19-20)

43. And Jesus said unto them, I am the bread of life: he that cometh to me SHALL NEVER HUNGER; and he that believeth on me SHALL NEVER THIRST. (ST. JOHN 6:35)

44. Verily, verily, I say unto you, he that believeth on me hath EVERLASTING LIFE. (ST. JOHN 6:47)

45. I am THAT bread of life. (ST. JOHN 6:48)

46. Whoso eateth my flesh, and drinketh my blood, hath eternal life and I WILL RAISE HIM UP at the last day. (ST. JOHN 6:54)

47. It is the spirit that quickened; the flesh profited nothing; the words I speak unto you, THEY ARE SPIRIT. and they are life. (ST. JOHN 6:63)

48. Jesus answered them, have not I chosen you twelve and ONE OF YOU IS A DEVIL? (ST. JOHN 6:70)

49. Jesus answered them, and said, my doctrine is not mine BUT HIS THAT SENT ME. (ST. JOHN 7:16)

50. But, lo, he speaketh boldly, and they say nothing unto him. Do the rulers know indeed that THIS IS THE VERY CHRIST? (ST. JOHN 7:26)

51. Then cried Jesus in the temple as he taught, saying, ye both know me, and ye know whence I am ; and I am not come of myself, but he that sent me is true, whom ye know not. But I KNOW HIM; FOR I AM FROM HIM, and he hath sent me. (ST. JOHN 7:28-29)

52. In the last day, that great day of the feast, Jesus stood and cried saying, if any man thirst, let him come unto me, and drink. He that believeth on me, as

the scripture hath said, out of his BELLY SHALL FLOW RIVER OF LIVING WATER. (ST. JOHN 7:37-38)

53. So when they continued asking him, he lifted up himself, and said unto them, he that is without sin among you, LET HIM FIRST CAST A STONE AT HER. And again he stooped down, and wrote on the ground. (ST. JOHN 8:7-8)

54. She said, no man, Lord. And Jesus said unto her, NEITHER DO I CONDEMN THEE, GO AND SIN NO MORE. (ST. JOHN 8:11)

55. Then Jesus spoke again unto them saying, I am the light of the world: he that followed me shall not walk in DARKNESS, but shall have the LIGHT OF LIFE. (ST. JOHN 8:12)

56. Then said they unto him, where is thy Father? Jesus answered, ye neither know me, nor my Father: if ye had known me, YE SHOULD HAVE KNOWN MY FATHER ALSO. (ST. JOHN 8:19)

57. Then said Jesus to those Jews which believed on him, if ye continue in my word, then are ye my disciples indeed. And ye shall know the truth, AND THE TRUTH SHALL MAKE YOU FREE. (ST. JOHN 8:31-32)

58. Your father Abraham rejoiced to see my day: AND HE SAW IT, AND WAS GLAD. (ST. JOHN 8:56)

59. Jesus said unto them, verily, verily, I say unto you, BEFORE ABRAHAM WAS, I AM. (ST. JOHN 8:58)

60. When he had thus spoken, HE SPAT ON THE GROUND, and made clay of the spittle, and he ANOINTED THE EYES of the blind man with clay. (ST. JOHN 9:6)

61. He answered and said, a man that is called Jesus made clay and anointed mine eyes, and said unto me, go to the pool of Siloam, and wash; and I went and washed, AND I RECEIVED SIGHT. (ST. JOHN 9:11)

62. But by what means he now seeth, we know not; or who hath opened his eyes, we know not; HE IS OF AGE, ASK HIM, HE SHALL SPEAK FOR HIMSELF. (ST. JOHN 9:21)

63. My sheep hear my voice, and I know them, AND THEY FOLLOW ME. And I give unto them eternal life; and they shall never perish, neither shall any man PLUCK THEM OUT OF MY HAND. My Father, which gave them me, is greater than all and NO MAN IS ABLE to pluck them out of my Father's hand. I and my Father are ONE. (ST. JOHN 10:27-30)

64. If I do not the works of my Father, believe me not. But if I do, though ye believe not me BELIEVE THE WORKS; that ye may know, and believe, that the FATHER IS IN ME, AND I IN HIM. (ST. JOHN 10:37-38)

65. Then said Jesus unto them plainly, Lazarus is dead. And I am glad for your sakes that I was not there, TO THE INTENT YOU MAY BELIEVE; nevertheless let us go into him. (ST. JOHN 11:14-15)

66. Then when Jesus came, he found that he had LAID IN THE GRAVE FOUR DAYS ALREADY. (ST. JOHN 11:17)

67. Martha saith unto him, I know that he shall rise again in the resurrection at the last day. Jesus said unto her, I AM THE RESURRECTION, and the life; he that believeth in me, though he were dead, YET SHALL HE LIVE. And whosoever liveth and believeth in me SHALL NEVER DIE. (ST. JOHN 11:24-26)

68. When Jesus therefore saw her weeping, and the Jews also weeping which came with her, HE GROANED IN THE SPIRIT, AND WAS TROUBLED. (ST. JOHN 11:33)

69. Jesus wept. (ST. JOHN 10:35)

70. Then they took away the stone from the place where the dead was laid. And Jesus lifted up his eyes, and said Father, I thank thee that thou hast heard me. And I knew that thou hearest me always; BUT BECAUSE OF THE PEOPLE which stand by I said it, that they may BELIEVE that thou hast sent me. And when he thus had spoken, he cried with a loud voice, LAZARUS, COME FORTH. And he that was dead came forth, bound hand and foot with graveclothes and his face was bound about with a napkin. Jesus said unto them, LOOSE HIM AND LET HIM GO. (ST. JOHN 11:41-44)

71. Father, glorify thy name. then came there a voice from heaven, saying, I have both glorified it and will glorify it again. The people therefore, that stood

by, and heard it, SAID THAT IT THUNDERED; others said, an angel spake to him. Jesus answered and said, this voice came not because of me, BUT FOR YOUR SAKES. Now is the judgement of this world; now shall the prince of this world be cast out. And I, if I be lifted up from the earth, WILL DRAW ALL MEN UNTO ME. (ST. JOHN 12:28-32)

72. Now before the feast of the Passover, when Jesus knew that his hour was come that he should depart out of this world unto the Father, having loved his own which were in the world, he loved them unto the end. And supper being ended, THE DEVIL having now put into the HEART OF JUDAS ISCARIOT, Simon's son, BETRAY HIM. (ST. JOHN 13:1-2)

73. If ye know these things, happy are ye IF YE DO THEM. (ST. JOHN 13:17)

74. When Jesus had thus said, he was troubled in spirit, and testified, and said, verily, verily, I say unto you, that one of you SHALL BETRAY ME. (ST. JOHN 13:21)

75. A new commandment I give unto you, that ye love one another; as I have loved you, THAT YE ALSO LOVE ONE ANOTHER. (ST. JOHN 13:34)

76. Let not your heart be troubled; ye believe in God, BELIEVE ALSO IN ME. (ST. JOHN 14:1)

77. Jesus saith unto him, I am the way, the truth and the life; NO MAN COMETH UNTO THE FATHER, BUT BY ME. (ST. JOHN 14:6)

78. And whatsoever ye shall ask in my name, THAT WILL I DO, that the Father may be glorified in the Son. If ye shall ask any thing in my name, I WILL DO IT. If ye love me, KEEP MY COMMANDMENTS. And I will pray the Father, and he shall give you another COMFORTER, that he may abide with you for ever. (ST. JOHN 14:13-16)

79. But the Comforter, which is the HOLY GHOST whom the Father will send in my name, he shall teach you all things, and BRING ALL THINGS TO YOUR REMEMBRANCE, whatsoever I have said unto you. (ST. JOHN 14:26)

80. I am the vine, ye are the branches: he that abideth in me and I in him, the same bringeth forth much fruit for without me YE CAN DO NOTHING. (ST. JOHN 15:5)

81. If ye abide in me, and my words abide in you, ye shall ask what ye will, and IT SHALL BE DONE UNTO YOU. (ST. JOHN 15:7)

82. These things have I spoken unto you, that my JOY might remain in you, and that your joy MIGHT BE FULL. (ST. JOHN 15:11)

83. And ye all shall bear witness, because ye have been with me FROM THE BEGINNING. (ST. JOHN 15:27)

84. Nevertheless I tell you the truth; it is expedient for you that I go away: for if I go not away THE COMFORTER WILL NOT COME UNTO YOU, but if I depart, I will send him unto you. (ST. JOHN 16:7)

85. Howbeit when he, the Spirit of Truth, is come, he will guide you into all truth: for he SHALL NOT SPEAK OF HIMSELF; but whatsoever he shall hear, THAT SHALL HE SPEAK; and he will show you things to come. (ST. JOHN 16:13)

86. Verily, verily, I say unto you, that ye shall weep and lament, but the world shall rejoice and ye shall be sorrowful, BUT YOUR SORROW SHALL BE TURNED INTO JOY. (ST. JOHN 16:20)

87. A woman when she is in travail hath sorrow, because her hour is come; but as soon as she is delivered of the child, SHE REMEMBERED NO MORE THE ANGUISH for joy that a man is born into the world. (ST. JOHN 16:21)

88. And in that day ye shall ask me nothing. Verily, verily, I say unto you, WHATSOEVER ye shall ask the Father IN MY NAME, he will give it you. (ST. JOHN 16:23)

89. At that day ye shall ask in my name; and I say not unto you, THAT I WILL PRAY the Father for you. (ST. JOHN 16:26)

90. For the Father himself loveth you, because ye have loved me, and have BELIEVED that I came OUT FROM GOD. (ST. JOHN 16:27)

91. As thou hast given him power over all flesh, that he should give eternal life to as many as thou hast given him. And this is life eternal, that they might

know thee the ONLY TRUE GOD AND JESUS CHRIST, whom thou hast sent. I have GLORIFIED thee on the earth; I have FINISHED THE WORK which thou gavest ME TO DO. (ST. JOHN 17:2-4)

92. Now they have known that all things whatsoever thou hast given me ARE OF THEE. (ST. JOHN 17:7)

93. I pray for them; I pray not for the world, but for them which thou hast given me; FOR THEY ARE THINE. (ST. JOHN 17:9)

94. While I was with them in the world, I kept them in thy name; those that thou gavest me I have kept, AND NONE OF THEM IS LOST but the Son of perdition; that the scripture might be fulfilled. (ST. JOHN 17:12)

95. I have given them thy word; and the world hath hated them, BECAUSE THEY ARE NOT OF THE WORLD even as I am not of the world. (ST. JOHN 17:14)

96. Sanctify them through thy truth; THY WORD IS TRUTH. (ST. JOHN 17:17)

97. And I have declared unto them thy name, and will declare it; that the love wherewith thou hast love me may be in them, AND I IN THEM. (ST. JOHN 17:26)

98. Then asked he them again, whom seek ye? And they said, JESUS OF NAZARETH. Jesus answered, I have told you that I AM HE; if therefore ye seek me, let these go their way; that the saying might be fulfilled, which he spake, of them which thou gavest me HAVE I LOST NONE. (ST. JOHN 18:7-9)

99. Jesus answered him, I spake openly to the world; I even taught in the synagogue, and in the temple, whither the Jews always resort, AND IN SECRET HAVE I SAID NOTHING. (ST. JOHN 18:20)

100. Peter then denied again; and IMMEDIATELY the cock crew. (ST. JOHN 18:27)

101. Then Pilate entered into the JUDGEMENT HALL AGAIN, and called Jesus, and said unto him, art thou the KING OF THE JEWS? (ST. JOHN 18:33)

102. Pilate saith unto him, what is truth? And when he had said this, he went out again unto the Jews, and saith unto them, I FIND IN HIM NO FAULT AT ALL. (ST. JOHN 18:38)

103. And the soldiers plaited a crown of thorns, and put it on his head, and they put on him A PURPLE ROLE. (ST. JOHN 19:2)

104. Jesus answered, thou couldest have no power at all against me, EXCEPT IT WERE GIVEN THEE FROM ABOVE; therefore he that delivered me unto thee hath THE GREATER SIN. (ST. JOHN 19:11)

105. When Jesus therefore had received the vinegar, he said IT IS FINISHED; and he bowed his head, and gave up the ghost. (ST. JOHN 19:30)

106. But when they came to Jesus, and saw that he was dead already, THEY BRAKE NOT HIS LEGS. But one of the soldiers with a spear pierced his side, and forthwith came there out BLOOD AND WATER. (ST. JOHN 19:33-34)

107. For these things were done, that the scripture should be fulfilled, A BONE OF HIM SHALL NOT BE BROKEN. And again another scripture saith, they shall look on him whom they pierced. (ST. JOHN 19:36-37)

108. And the napkin, that was about his head, not lying with the linen clothes, but wrapped together IN A PLACE BY ITSELF. (ST. JOHN 20:7)

109. But Mary stood without at the sepulchre weeping: and as she wept, she stooped down and looked into the scpulchre, and seeth TWO ANGLES IN WHITE, sitting, the one at the HEAD, and the other at the FEET where the body of Jesus had lain. And they say unto her, Woman, why weepest thou? She saith unto them, because they have TAKEN AWAY MY LORD, and I know not where they laid him. And when she had thus said she turned herself back, AND SAW JESUS STANDING, and knew not that it was Jesus. (ST. JOHN 20:11-14)

110. Jesus saith unto her, TOUCH ME NOT, for I am not yet ascended to my Father; but go to my brethren, and say unto them, I ASCEND UNTO MY FATHER, and your Father; and to MY GOD and your God. (ST. JOHN 20:17)

111. And when he had so said, he showed unto them HIS HANDS AND HIS SIDE.   Then were the disciples glad, when they saw the Lord. (ST. JOHN 20:20)

112. And when he had said this, HE BREATHED ON THEM and saith unto them, receive ye THE HOLY GHOST. (ST. JOHN 20:22)

113. But Thomas, one of the twelve, called Didymus, was not with them when JESUS CAME. (ST. JOHN 20:24)

114. Jesus saith unto him, THOMAS because thou hast seen me, thou hast believed: Blessed are they that have NOT SEEN, AND YET HAVE BELIEVED. (ST. JOHN 20:29)

115. This is now the third time that Jesus showed himself to his disciples, after that he WAS RISEN FROM THE DEAD. (ST. JOHN 21:14)

116. Peter seeing him saith to Jesus, Lord, and what shall this man do? Jesus saith unto him, if I will that he tarry till I come, what is that to thee? FOLLOW ME. (ST. JOHN 21:22)

117. And there are also many other things, WHICH JESUS DID, the which, if they should be written every one, I suppose that even THE WORLD ITSELF could not contain THE BOOKS THAT SHOULD BE WRITTEN. AMEN. (ST. JOHN 21:25

THE END ST. JOHN

ACTS

1. And being assembled together with them, commanded with them, commanded them that THEY SHOULD NOT DEPART FROM JERUSALEM, BUT WAIT for the promise of the Father, which, saith he, ye have heard of me. For John truly baptized with water; but ye shall be baptized WITH THE HOLY GHOST, not many days hence. (ACTS 1:4-5)

2. But ye shall receive power, after that the Holy Ghost is come upon you: and ye shall be witness unto me both in JERUSALEM, and in all JUDAEA, and in SAMARIA, and unto the uttermost part of the earth! And when he had spoken these things, while they beheld, he was taken up; and a cloud RECEIVE HIM OUT OF THEIR SIGHT. And while they looked steadfastly toward heaven as he went up, behold, two men stood by them in white apparel; which also said, ye men of Galilee, why stand ye gazing up into heaven? This same Jesus, which is taken up from you into heaven, SHALL SO COME IN LIKE MANNER as ye have seen him go into heaven. (ACTS 1:8-11)

3. And they prayed and said, thou, Lord, which knowest the hearts of ALL MEN, show whether of these TWO thou has chosen. (ACTS 1:24)

4. And they gave forth their lots; and the lot fell upon MATTHIAS; and he was numbered with the ELEVEN APOSTLES. (ACTS 1:26)

5. And when the day of Pentecost was fully come, they were all with ONE ACCORD IN ONE PLACE. (ACTS 2:1)

6. And suddenly there came a sound from heaven as of a RUSHING MIGHTY WIND, and it filled all the house where they were sitting. (ACTS 2:2)

7. And they were all filled with the HOLY GHOST, and began to speak with OTHER TONGUES, as the Spirit gave them utterance. (ACTS 2:4)

8. Others mocking said, these men are full of new WINE. (ACTS 2:13)

9. And it shall come to pass in the last days, saith God, I WILL POUR OUT OF MY SPIRIT UPON ALL FLESH; and your sons and your daughters SHALL PROPHESY, and your young men shall see VISIONS, and your old men shall DREAM DREAMS. (ACTS 2:17)

10. And it shall come to pass, that whosoever shall call on the name of the Lord SHALL BE SAVED. (ACTS 2:21)

11. Then Peter said unto them, repent and be baptized every one of you in the name of Jesus Christ for the remission of sins, and ye shall receive the GIFT OF THE HOLY GHOST. (ACTS 2:38)

12. And with many other words did he testify and exhort, saying, save yourselves from this UNTOWARD GENERATION. (ACTS 2:40)

13. Then they that gladly received his word were BAPTIZED; and the same day there were added unto them about THREE THOUSAND SOULS. (ACTS 2:41)

14. And all that believed were together, and had all things COMMON. (ACTS 2:44)

15. And a certain man lame from his mother's womb was carried, whom they laid daily at the gate of the temple which is called BEAUTIFUL, to ask alms of them that entered into the temple. (ACTS 3:2)

16. Then Peter said, silver and gold have I none; BUT SUCH AS I HAVE GIVE I THEE in the name of Jesus Christ of Nazareth RISE UP AND WALK. And he took him by the right hand and lifted him up; and immediately his feet and ankle bones RECEIVED STRENGTH. (ACTS 3:6-7)

17. But ye denied the Holy One and the Just, and desired a murderer to be granted unto you. And killed the Prince of life, who God hath raised from the dead whereof we are witness. And his name THROUGH FAITH IN HIS NAME hath made this man strong, whom ye see and know; yea, THE FAITH which is by him hath given him this perfect soundness in the presence of you all. (ACTS 3:14-16)

18. Ye are the children of the prophet, and of the covenant which God made with our fathers, saying, UNTO ABRAHAM, and in thy seed shall all the kindreds of the earth BE BLESSED. (ACTS 3:25)

19. And they laid hands on them, and put them in hold UNTIL THE NEXT DAY; for it was now eventide. (ACTS 4:3)

20. Now when they saw the boldness of Peter and John, and perceived that they were unlearned and ignorant men, they marvelled; and they took knowledge of them, that they had   BEING WITH JESUS. (ACTS 4:13)

21. And they called them and commanded them not to speak at all nor teach IN THE NAME OF JESUS. (ACTS 4:18)

22. So when they had further threatened them, they let them go finding nothing how they might punish them, because of the people FOR ALL MEN GLORIFIED GOD for that which was done. (ACTS 4:21)

23. And when they heard that, they lifted up their voice TO GOD WITH ONE ACCORD and said Lord, thou art God, which hast made HEAVEN AND EARTH AND THE SEA, and all that in them is. (ACTS 4:24)

24. And laid them down at the apostles' feet; and DISTRIBUTION was made unto every man ACCORDING AS HE HAD NEED. (ACTS 4:35)

25. But a certain man named Ananias, with Sapphira, his wife, sold a possession. And KEPT BACK PART of the price, his wife also being privy to it, and brought a certain part, AND LAID IT AT THE APOSTLE'S FEET. But Peter said Ananias why hath Satan filled thine heart TO LIE TO THE HOLY GHOST, and to keep back part of the price of the land. (ACTS 5:1-3)

26. And Ananias hearing these words fell down, and GAVE UP THE GHOST; and great fear came on all them that heard these things. (ACTS 5:5)

27. And it was about the space of three hours after, when his wife, not knowing wat was done, CAME IN. (ACTS 5:7)

28. Then Peter said unto her, how is it that ye have agreed together to tempt THE SPIRIT OF THE LORD? Behold, the feet of them which have buried thy husband ARE AT THE DOOR, and shall carry thee out. Then fell she down straightway at his feet, and YIELDED UP THE GHOST; and the young men came in, and found her dead, and, carrying her forth BURIED HER BY HER HUSBAND. (ACTS 5:9-10)

29. Insomuch that they brought forth the sick into the streets, and laid them on beds and couches, that at the least the SHADOW OF PETER PASSING BY might overshadow some of them. (ACTS 5:15)

30. And laid their hands on the apostles and put them in the common PRISON. But the angel of the Lord by night OPENED THE PRISON DOORS, and brought them forth and said, go, stand and speak in the temple to the people all the words of this life. (ACTS 5:18-20)

31. Then Peter and the other apostles answered and said, WE OUGHT TO OBEY GOD RATHER THAN MAN. (ACTS 5:29)

32. And we are his witness of these things, and so is also THE HOLY GHOST, whom God hath given to them THAT OBEY HIM. (ACTS 5:32)

33. And daily in the temple, and in every house, they ceased not to teach and preach JESUS CHRIST. (ACTS 5:42)

34. And Stephen, full of faith and power, did great wonders and miracles AMONG THE PEOPLE. (ACTS 6:8)

35. And they were not able to resist the WISDOM AND THE SPIRIT by which he spake. (ACTS 6:10)

36. And all that sat in the council, looking steadfastly on him, saw his face as it had been THE FACE OF AN ANGEL. (ACTS 6:15)

37. And he gave him the Covenant of Circumcision and so ABRAHAM BEGAT ISAAC, and circumcised him the eighth day; and Isaac begat JACOB and Jacob begat THE TWELVE PATRIARCH. (ACTS 7:8)

38. And the patriarchs, moved with envy, sold Joseph into Egypt; BUT GOD WAS WITH HIM. (ACTS 7:9)

39. In which time Moses was born, and was exceeding fair, and nourished up in his father's house THREE MONTHS; and when he was cast out, PHARAOH'S DAUGHTER took him up and nourished him for her OWN SON. (ACTS 7:20-21)

40. And when he was full forty years old, it came into his heart to visit his brethren the CHILDREN OF ISRAEL. (ACTS 7:23)

41. Wilt thou kill me, as thou didest the Egyptian yesterday? Then FLED Moses at this saying, and was a stranger in the land of MADIAN where he begat TWO SONS. And when forty years were expired, there appeared to in

the wilderness of Mount Sina, an angel of the Lord in a FLAME OF FIRE IN A BUSH. When Moses saw it, he wondered at the sight; and as he drew near to behold it THE VOICE OF THE LORD CAME UNTO HIM, Saying, I am the God of thy fathers, the God of Abraham, and the father of Isaac, and the God of Jacob. Then Moses trembled, and durst not behold. Then said the Lord to him, PUT OFF THY SHOES FROM THY FEET; FOR THE PLACE WHERE THOU STANDEST IS HOLY GROUND. (ACTS 7:28-33)

42. But he, being full of the Holy Ghost, looked up steadfast into heaven, and saw the glory of God, and JESUS STANDING ON THE RIGHT HAND OF GOD. (ACTS 7:55)

43. And cast him out of the city and STONED HIM and the witness laid down their clothes at a young man's feet, WHOSE NAME WAS SAUL. (ACTS 7:58)

44. And they stoned Stephen, calling upon God, and saying, Lord Jesus receive my spirit and he kneeled down, and cried with a loud voice, LORD LAY NOT THIS SIN TO THEIR CHARGE. And when he had said this, he fell asleep. (ACTS 7:59-60)

45. And Saul was consenting unto his death. And at that time there was GREAT PERSECUTION AGAINST THE CHURCH which was at Jerusalem; and they were all scattered abroad throughout the regions of JUDAEA AND SAMARIA except the apostles. (ACTS 8:1)

46. As for Saul, he made havoc of the church, entering into every house, AND HALING MEN AND WOMEN committed them to prison. (ACTS 8:3)

47. But there was a certain man, called Simon, which beforetime in the same city used sorcery and bewitched the people of Samaria, giving out that himself was some GREAT ONE. (ACTS 8:9)

48. And when Simon saw that through laying on of the apostles' hands the Holy Ghost was given, he OFFERED THEM MONEY. (ACTS 8:18)

49. But Peter said unto him, thy money PERISH with thee, because thou hast thought that the GIFT OF GOD may be purchased with money. (ACTS 8:20)

50. Repent therefore of this thy wickedness, and pray God, if perhaps the THOUGHT OF THINE HEART may be forgiven thee. (ACTS 8:22)

51. Then the Spirit said, unto Phillip, go near, and join thyself to this CHARIOT. (ACTS 8:29)

52. And Phillip said, if thou believest with all thine heart thou mayest. And he answered and said, I BELIEVE THAT JESUS CHRIST IS THE SON OF GOD. And he commanded the chariot to STAND STILL; and they went down, both into the water, both Philip and the eunuch; and he BAPTIZED HIM. And when they were come up out of the water, THE SPIRIT OF THE LORD CAUGHT AWAY PHILIP, that the eunuch saw him no more; and he went on his way rejoicing. (ACTS 8:37-39)

53. And as he journeyed, he came near Damascus and suddenly there shined round about him A LIGHT FROM HEAVEN. And he fell to the earth, and heard a voice saying unto him Saul, SAUL, WHY PERSECUTEST ME? (ACTS 9:3-4)

54. And he was three days WITHOUT SIGHT, and neither did eat nor drink. (ACTS 9:9)

55. And there was a certain disciple at DAMARCUS NAMED ANANIAS, and to him said the Lord in a vision, Ananias. And he said, behold, I AM HERE LORD. (ACTS 9:10)

56. But the Lord said unto him, go thy way; FOR HE IS A CHOSEN VESSEL UNTO ME, to bear my name before the Gentiles, and kings and the children of Israel. (ACTS 9:15)

57. And immediately there fell from his eyes as it had been SCALES; and he received SIGHT forthwith, and arose, and was BAPTIZED. (ACTS 9:18)

58. And straightway he preached Christ in the synagogues, that he is the SON OF GOD. (ACTS 9:20)

59. And after that many days were fulfilled, the Jews took COUNSEL TO KILL HIM. (ACTS 9:23)

60. Then the disciples took him by night, and let him down by the WALL IN A BASKET. (ACTS 9:25)

61. But Barnabus took him, and brought him to the apostles, and declared unto them how he had seen the Lord in the way and that he had spoken to him and how he had PREACHED BOLDLY at Damascus in the NAME OF JESUS. (ACTS 9:27)

62. But Peter put them all forth, and kneeled down, and prayed; and turning him to the body said Tabitha, arise. And she opened her eyes; and when she saw Peter, SHE SAT UP. (ACTS 9:40)

63. He saw in a vision evidently about the nineth hour of the day AN ANGEL OF GOD COMING IN TO HIM, and saying unto him, Cornelius, and when he looked on him, he was afraid, and said, what is it Lord? And he said unto him, THY PRAYERS AND THINE ALMS ARE COME UP FOR A MEMORIAL BEFORE GOD. (ACTS 10:3-4)

64. And when he had declared all these things unto them, he sent THEM TO JOPPA. (ACTS 10:8)

65. And he became very hungry, and would have eaten; but while they made ready, HE FELL INTO A TRANCE. (ACTS 10:10)

66. And the voice spake unto him again the second time, what God hath cleansed, THAT CALL NOT THOU COMMON. (ACTS 10:15)

67. While Peter thought on the vision, the Spirit said unto him, behold, three men seek thee. Arise therefore, and get thee down, and go with them DOUBTING NOTIHING; FOR I HAVE SENT THEM. (ACTS 10:19-20)

68. But Peter took him up, saying, stand up; I MYSELF ALSO AM A MAN. (ACTS 10:26)

69. But in every nation he that feareth him and worketh righteousness is accepted WITH HIM. (ACTS 10:35)

70. To him give all the prophets witness, that through his name whosoever believeth in him SHALL RECEIVE REMISSION OF SINS. While Peter yet spake these words, THE HOLY GHOST fell on all them which heard the word. (ACTS 10:43-44)

71. Can any man forbid water, that these should not be baptized, which have received THE HOLY GHOST AS WELL AS WE? (ACTS 10:47)

72. And as I began to speak, the Holy Ghost fell on them, as on us at the beginning. Then remembered I the word of the Lord, how that he said, John indeed baptized with water, but ye shall be baptized with the Holy Ghost. Forasmuch then as God gave them the like gift as he did unto us, WHO BELIEVED ON THE LORD JESUS CHRIST; what was I, that I could withstand God? When they heard these things, they held their peace, and glorified God saying, THEN HAS GOD ALSO TO THE GENTILES GRANTED REPENTANCE UNTO LIFE. Now they which were scattered abroad upon the persecution that arose about STEPHEN traveled as far as Phenice, and Cyprus, and Antioch PREACHING THE WORD TO NONE BUT UNTO THE JEWS ONLY. (ACTS 11:15-19)

73. And he killed James the brother of John with the SWORD. (ACTS 12:2)

74. Peter therefore was kept in prison: but prayers was made WITHOUT CEASING of the church unto GOD FOR HIM. (ACTS 12:5)

75. And when Herod would have brought him forth, the same night PETER WAS SLEEPING between two soldiers, bound with two chains: and the keepers before the kept the prison. (ACTS 12:6)

76. And , behold, the angel of the Lord came upon him and a light shined in the prison; and he smote Peter on the side and raised him up saying, ARISE UP QUICKLY. AND HIS CHAINS FELL OFF FROM HIS HANDS. (ACTS 12:7)

77. And when Peter was come to himself, he said, now I know of a surety, that the Lord hath SENT HIS ANGELS And hath delivered me out of the hand of Herod, and from all the EXPECTATION of the people of the Jews.   (ACTS 12:11)

78. And upon a set day Herod arrayed in royal apparel, sat upon his throne, and made an oration unto them. And the people gave a shout, saying, it is the voice of a god, and not of a man. And immediately THE ANGEL OF THE LORD smote him, because he gave not God the glory; AND HE WAS EATEN OF WORMS, AND gave up the ghost.(ACTS 12:21-23

79. And when they had gone through the isle unto Paphos, they found a certain sorcerer, A FALSE PROPHET, a Jew, whose name as BAR-JESUS. (ACTS 13:6)

80. Then Saul, (who also is called Paul) filled with the Holy Ghost, SET HIS EYES ON HIM. (ACTS 13:9)

81. And now, behold, the hand of the Lord is upon thee, and thou shalt be blind, NOT SEEING THE SUN FOR A SEASON. And immediately there fell on him A MIST AND A DARKNESS and he went about seeking some to LEAD HIM BY THE HAND. (ACTS 13:11)

82. Then Paul stood up, and beckoning with his hands said, men of Israel, and ye that fear God, GIVE AUDIENCE. (ACTS 13:16)

83. And when he had removed him, he raised up unto them David to be their king; to whom also he gave testimony, and said, I have found David, the son of Jesse, a man after mine own heart, WHICK SHALL FULFILL ALL MY WILL. (ACTS 13:22)

84. And as John fulfilled his course, he said, whom think ye that I am? I am not he. But behold, there cometh one after me, WHOSE SHOES OF HIS FEET I AM NOT WORTHY TO LOOSE. (ACTS 13:25)

85. And by him all that believe are justified from all things, from which ye could not be justified BY THE LAW OF MOSES. (ACTS 13:39)

86. And the next Sabbath day came almost the whole city together to hear the word of GOD. But when the Jews saw the multitudes, they were filled with ENVY, and spake against those things which were spoken by PAUL contradicting and blaspheming. (ACTS 13:44-45)

87. But they shook off the dust of their feet AGAINST THEM, and came unto Iconium. ACTS 13:51)

88. But the unbelieving Jews stirred up the Gentiles, and MADE THEIR MINDS EVIL affected against the brethren. (ACTS 14:2)

89. They were ware of it, and fled unto Lystra and Derbe, cities of Lycaonia, and unto the region that lieth round about; and there they PREACHED THE

GOSPEL. And there sat a certain man at Lystra, impotent in his feet, being a cripple from his mother's womb, WHO NEVER HAD WALKED. The same heard Paul speak; who steadfastly beholding him, and preceiving that he had FAITH TO BE HEALED, said in a loud voice, stand upright on thy feet. AND HE LEAPED AND WALKED. (ACTS 14:6-10)

90. And there came thither certain Jews from Antioch and Iconium, who persuaded the people, and , having STONED PAUL, drew him out of the city, SUPPOSING HE HAD BEEN DEAD. (ACTS 14:19)

91. And when they had ordained them elders in every church, and had prayed with fasting, they COMMENDED THEM TO THE LORD, on whom they believe. (ACTS 14:23)

92. And God, which knoweth the hearts, bare them witness, giving them the Holy Ghost, even as he did unto us. And put no difference between us and them, PURIFYING THEIR HEARTS BY FAITH. (ACTS 15:8-9)

93. And they wrote letters by them after this manner; THE APOSTLES AND ELDERS AND BRETHREN SEND GREETING unto the brethren which are of the Gentiles in Antioch and Syria and Cilicia. (ACTS 15:23)

94. For it seemed good to the Holy Ghost, and to us, to lay upon you NO GREATER BURDEN THAN THESE NECESSARY THINGS. That ye abstain from meats offered to idols, and from blood, and from things strangled, and from fornication; from which if ye keep yourselves, ye shall do well. Fare ye well. (ACTS 15:28-29)

95. And the contention was so sharp between them that THEY DEPARTED ASUNDER ONE FROM THE OTHER; and so Barnabus took Mark, and sailed unto Cyprus. And Paul chose SILAS AND DEPARTED, being recommend by the brethren unto the grace of God. (ACTS 15:39-40)

96. The same followed Paul and us, and cried, saying, these men are the servants of the most High God, which show unto us the way of salvation. And this did she many days. BUT PAUL, BEING GRIEVED, TURNED AND SAID TO THE SPIRIT, I command thee in the name of Jesus Christ to come out of her. And he came out the same hour. (ACTS 16:17-18)

97. And when they had laid many stripes upon them, THEY CAST THEM INTO PRISON, charging the jailer to keep them safety. (ACTS 16:23)

98. And at midnight Paul and Silas prayed and sang praises unto God AND THE PRISONERS HEARD THEM. (ACTS 16:25)

99. But Paul cried with a loud voice, saying, do thyself no harm; FOR WE ARE ALL HERE. (ACTS 16:28)

100. And they came and besought them, and brought them out, and desired them to depart OUT OF THE CITY. (ACTS 16:39)

101. And then immediately the brethren sent away Paul to go as it were to the sea; BUT SILAS AND TIMOTHEUS ABODE THERE STILL. (ACTS 17:14)

102. Now while Paul waited for them at Athens, his spirit was stirred in him, when he saw the city WHOLLY GIVEN TO IDOLATRY. (ACTS 17:16)

103. For as I passed by, and beheld your devotions, I found an altar with this inscription, TO THE UNKNOWN GOD. Whom therefore ye ignorantly worship, him declare I unto you. God that made the world and ALL THINGS THEREIN, seeing that he is Lord of heaven and earth, dwelleth NOT IN temples made with hands. (ACTS 17:23-24)

104. For in him we live, and move, and have our being; as certain also of your own poets have said, FOR WE ARE ALSO HIS OFFSPRING. (ACTS 17:28)

105. And the times of this ignorance God winked at; but now commandeth ALL MEN EVERY WHERE TO REPENT. (ACTS 17:30)

106. So Paul DEPARTED from among them. (ACTS 17:33)

107. Then spake the Lord to Paul in the night BY A VISION, be not afraid, but speak, and HOLD NOT THY PEACE; for I am with thee, and no man shall set on thee to hurt thee; for I have much people in this city. (ACTS 18:9-10)

108. And Paul after this tarried there yet a good while, and then took his leave of the brethren, and sailed thence into Syria and with him PRISCILLA AND AQUILA having shorn his head in Cenchrea, FOR HE HAD A VOW. (ACTS 18:18)

109. And he began to speak boldly in the synagogue; whom when Aquila and Priscilla had heard, THEY TOOK HIM UNTO THEM, and expounded unto him the way of GOD MORE PERFECTLY. (ACTS 18:26)

110. Then said Paul, John verily baptized with the baptism of repentance, saying unto the people, that they should believe on him which should COME AFTER HIM, that is, on Jesus Christ. When they heard this, they were baptized IN THE NAME OF LORD JESUS and when Paul had laid his hands upon them, THE HOLY GHOST CAME UPON THEM; and they spake with tongues, and prophesied. And all the men were about TWELVE. (ACTS 19:4-7)

111. And the evil spirit answered and said, Jesus I know, and Paul I know; BUT WHO ARE YE? And the man in whom the evil spirit was leaped on them and overcame them, and prevailed against them, so that they fled out of that house NAKED AND WOUNDED. (ACTS 19:15-16)

112. And many that believed came, and confessed, and showed THEIR DEEDS. (ACTS 19:18)

113. Some therefore, cried one thing, and some another: for the ASSEMBLY WAS CONFUSED; and the more part knew not wherefore they were come together. (ACTS 19:23)

114. For we are in danger to be called in question for this day's uproar. There being no cause whereby we may give an account of this concourse. And when he had thus spoken, HE DISMISSED THE ASSEMBLY. (ACTS 19:40-41)

115. And there sat in a window a certain young man named Eutychus, being fallen into a deep sleep; and as Paul was long preaching, he sunk down with sleep and FELL DOWN FROM THE THIRD LOFT and was taken up dead. And Paul went down, and fell on him, and embracing him said, trouble not yourselves ; FOR HIS LIFE IS IN HIM. (ACTS 20:9-10)

116. And now, behold, I know that ye all among whom I have gone preaching the kingdom of God SHALL SEE MY FACE NO MORE wherefore, I take you to record this day that I am pure from the BLOOD OF ALL MEN. For I have not shunned to declare unto you all the counsel of God. Take heed therefore unto yourselves, and to all the flock, over the which THE HOLY GHOST HATH MADE YOU OVERSEERS, to feed the church of God, which he hath purchased WITH HIS OWN BLOOD. (ACTS 20:25-28)

117. I have shown you all things, how that so labouring ye ought to support the weak, and remember the words of the Lord Jesus, how he said, it is more BLESSED TO GIVE THAN TO RECEIVE. (ACTS 20:35)

118. And when he had thus spoken he kneeled down and prayed with them all. And they all wept sore, and FELL ON PAUL'S NECK and kissed him. Sorrowing most of all for the words which he spake that they should see his face NO MORE. And they accompanied him unto the ship. (ACTS 20:36-38)

119. And finding disciples, we tarried there seven days: who said to Paul through the spirit, that he SHOULD NOT go up to Jerusalem. (ACTS 21:4)

120. Then Paul answered, What mean ye to weep and to break mine heart? For I am ready not to be bound only, but also TO DIE AT JERUSALEM for the name of the Lord Jesus. (ACTS 21:13)

121. And when the seven days were almost ended, the Jews which were Asia, when they saw him IN THE TEMPLE, stirred up all the people, and LAID HANDS ON HIM. (ACTS 21:27)

122. And as they went about to kill him, tidings came unto the chief captain of the band, that ALL JERUSALEM WAS IN AN UPROAR. (ACTS 21:31)

123. And when he had given him license, Paul stood on the stairs and beckoned with the hand unto the people. And when there was made a great silence, HE SPAKE UNTO THEM IN THE HEBREW TONGUE saying, men, brethren, and fathers, hear ye MY DEFENSE which I make now unto you. (ACTS 21:40 AND 22:1)

124. I am verily a man which am a Jew, born in Tarsus, a city in Cilicia, yet brought up in this city at the feet of Gamaliel, and TAUGHT ACCORDING to the perfect manner of the LAW OF THE FATHERS, and was zealous toward God, as ye all are this day. (ACTS 22:3)

125. And I answered, who art thou Lord? And he said unto me, I am Jesus of Nazareth, WHOM THOU PERSECUTES. (ACTS 22:8)

126. And I said, What shall I do Lord? And the Lord said unto me, arise, and go into Damascus; and there it shall be told thee of ALL THINGS WHICH ARE APPOINTED FOR THEE TO DO. (ACTS 22:10)

127. Came unto me, and stood, and said unto me Brother Saul, receive thy sight and the SAME HOUR I LOOKED UP UPON HIM. (ACTS 22:13)

128. And now why tarriest thou? Arise, and be baptized, and WASH AWAY THY SINS, calling on the name of the Lord. (ACTS 22:16)

129. And when the blood of thy martyr STEPHEN WAS SHED, I ALSO WAS STANDING BY, and consenting unto his death and kept the raiment of them that slew him. (ACTS 22:20)

130. And when he had so said, there arose a dissension between the Pharisees and the Sadducees: AND THE MULTITUDE WAS DIVIDED. (ACTS 23:7)

131. And there arose a great cry; and the scribes that were of the Pharisees' part arose, and strove saying, WE FIND NO EVIL IN THIS MAN; but if a spirit or an angel hath spoken to him, LET US NOT FIGHT AGAINST GOD. (ACTS 23:9)

132. So the chief captain then let the young man depart, AND CHARGED HIM, see thou tell no man that thou hast shown hast shown THESE THINGS TO ME. (ACTS 23:22)

133. But this I confess unto thee, that after the way which they call heresy, so worship I the God of my fathers, believing all things which are written in the law and in the prophets; and have hope toward God, which they themselves also allow, that THERE SHALL BE A RESURRECTION OF THE DEAD, BOTH OF THE JUST AND UNJUST. And herein do I exercise myself, to have always a conscience VOID OF OFFENCE, toward God and toward men. (ACTS 24:14-16)

134. And as he reasoned of righteousness, temperance, and judgement to come, Felix trembled. And answered, GO THY WAY FOR THIS TIME; when I have a convenience season, I WILL CALL FOR THEE. (ACTS 24:25)

135. Then said Paul, I stand at Caesar's judgement seat, where I ought to be judged: TO THE JEWS HAVE I DONE NO WRONG as thou very well knowest. (ACTS 25:10)

136. Then Festur, when he had conferred with the council, answered, Hast thou appealed unto Caesar? UNTO CAESAR SHALT THOU GO. (ACTS 25:12)

137. But when I found that he had committed nothing worthy of death, and that he himself hath appealed to Augustus, I HAVE DETERMINED TO SEND HIM. (ACTS 25:25)

138. For it seemeth to me unreasonable TO SEND A PRISONER and not withal to signify the crimes laid against him. (ACTS 25:27)

139. At midday, O king, I saw in the way A LIGHT FROM HEAVEN, ABOVE THE BRIGHTNESS OF THE SUN, shinning round about me and them which journeyed with me. (ACTS 26:13)

140. But rise, and stand upon thy feet; for I have appeared unto thee f or this purpose, TO MAKE THEE A MINISTER AND A WITNESS both of these things which thou hast seen, and of those things in the which I will appear unto thee. (ACTS 26:16)

141. To open their eyes, and turn them from DARKNESS TO LIGHT and from the power of Satan unto God, that they may receive forgiveness of sins, and inheritance among them which are sanctified BY FAITH THAT IS IN ME. (ACTS 26:18)

142. The Agrippa said unto Paul, almost thou persuades ME TO BE A CHRISTIAN. (ACTS 26:28)

143. And when they were gone aside, they talked between themselves, saying, this man doeth NOTHING WORTHY OF DEATH OR OF BONDS. (ACTS 26:31)

144. And said unto them, sirs, I perceive that this voyage WILL BE WITH HURT AND MUCH DAMAGE. (ACTS 27:10)

145. But not long after there arose against it a tempestuous wind called EUROCLYDON. (ACTS 27:14)

146. But after long abstinence Paul stood forth in the midst of them, and said, sirs, ye should have HEARKENED UNTO ME, and not have loosed from crete, and to have gained this harm and loss. (ACTS 27:21)

147. And the rest, some on boards, and some on broken pieces of the ship. And so it came to pass, that they ESCAPED ALL SAFE TO LAND. (ACT 27:44)

148. And when Paul had gathered a bundle of sticks, and laid them on the fire, there came a VIPER out of the heat and fastened on his hand. (ACTS 28:3)

149. And he shook off the beast into the fire, and felt NO HARM. (ACTS 28:5)

150. Who, when they had examined me, would have let me go, because there was NO CAUSE OF DEATH IN ME. (ACTS 28:18)

151. And some believed the things which were spoken, AND SOME BELIEVED NOT . (ACTS 28:24)

152. And Paul dwelt two whole years in his own hired house, and received all that came in unto him. PREACHING THE KINGDOM OF GOD, AND TEACHING THOSE THINGS WHICH CONCERN the Lord Jesus Christ, with all confidence, no man forbidding him. (ACTS 28:30-31)

THE END THE ACTS

ESSAY - THE OLD TESTAMENT
(suggestions)
The Book of Genesis (6Q)

1. List each day 1-7, and describe what the Lord God did each day. Explain the difference between the tree of knowledge of good and evil and the tree of live.

2. Explain the circumstances around Abel's killing and what was the vengeance of God to Cain?

3. Give a vivid description of the Ark and how many peoples were saved. How many days did the water prevail upon the earth?

4. Who was Hagar and Ishmael? What was Ishmael's blessings?

5. Who was Jacob and Esau? Why did Esau hate Jacob? What were the circumstances regarding Jacob's wives, Leah and Rachel? Why did Jacob flee from Laban?

6. Who was Joseph's parents? Give accounts of Joseph's life from the time he was seventeen until his death.

The Book of Exodus (3Q)

1. Moses was a Hebrew, explain why he was reared by the Egyptian?

2. List at least five (5) of the plagues that was upon Pharaoh and his people.

3. List the Ten commandments

The Book of Leviticus (3Q)

1. Nabad and Abihu, the sons of Aaron, died before the Lord. Why? What did Moses say and what did Aaron say?

2. List some of the blessings for obedience and list some of the punishments for disobedience. (chapter 26)

3. What portion of tithes is holy unto the Lord?

The Book of Numbers (5Q)

1. What tribe was in charge over the tabernacle of testimony and all the vessels thereof?

2. What are the three vows of a Nazarite?

3. Why was the anger of the Lord kindled against Miriam and Aaron? What happened to Miriam?

4. The tithes of the Children of Israel, the Lord gave to the Levities. What were commanded by the Lord to the Levities and what part should be their tithes?

5. Moses saw the promised land from what mountain? Why didn't Moses make it to the promised land? Who was given charge over the Children of Israel to lead them to the promised land?

The Book of Deuteronomy (3Q)

1. Moses said unto them, Hear O'Isreal, the statutes and judgments which I speak into your ears this day, that ye may learn them, and keep them, and do them. The Lord our God made a Covenant with us in Horeb. What was that Covenant called? List at least five of them.

2. List the blessings of obedience. Read again the curses of disobedience.

3. Where did Moses die and where was he buried? How long did he live? Who had the charge of leading the Children of Israel to the promised land? How long did the Children of Israel wept for Moses?

THE END – ESSAY – THE OLD TESTAMENT

ESSAY - THE NEW TESTAMENT
(suggestions)
The Book of St. Matthew (5Q)

1. Who was John the Baptist? What clothing did he wear and what was his meat?

2. Explain the parable of the sower.

3. What defiles a man?

4. Jesus healed many. Matthew 9:18-22, Matthew 9:27-30 and Matthew 14:25-32 are three different healings. What did each of these healings have in common?

5. After the resurrection, what was the great commission given to the eleven disciples in Galilee and why is there only eleven disciples instead of twelve at this time?

The Book of St. Mark (5Q)

1. List the twelve ordained disciples.

2. List the sin that is in danger of eternal damnation because it cannot be forgiven.

3. The disciples had the power to cast out devils, however, they were unable to heal this demoniac boy which had a dumb spirit. Why?

4. Who betrayed Jesus and why? Who denied Jesus and how many times were he denied?

5. What color was Jesus clothed in after he was led away to be crucified?

The Book of St. Luke (6Q)
1. While Zacharias was standing in the altar of incense, an angel spake with him. Who was the angel; what was the message and the results of Zacharias' unbelief?

2. Describe the surrounding events of the birth of Jesus.

3. What was written in the book of the Prophet Esaias when Jesus opened it?

4. Jesus called his twelve disciples together and gave them power and authority over all devils, and to cure diseases. What was his commission to them at that gathering?

5. Describe the parable of the lost son.

6. Jesus opened their understanding, that they might understand the scriptures, why did he want them to tarry in Jerusalem?

The Book of St. John (7Q)

1. John the Baptist was sent from God to bear witness of Jesus. What was his message?

2. The scribes and Pharisees brought unto Jesus a woman taken in adultery, the very act. How did Jesus respond to the Pharisees?

3. What is the shortest verse in the Bible?

4. How did Jesus identify the disciple that was going to betray him?

5. In reference to the Crucifixion: what was the place called that they took Jesus? Who wrote the title on the cross and what did it say? How many languages were the title written in and name the languages.

6. After they had crucified Jesus, they took his garments and made four parts. What was the deciding factor that made the soldiers cast lot for Jesus' coat?

7. Which of the disciples was missing when Jesus returned after the resurrection? What did Jesus do to encourage him to have faith and to believe?

The Book of Acts (8Q)

1. Under what circumstances were Saul converted? What did Saul's name change to after the conversion?

2. Explain Peter's trance and what was his vision?

3. Peter was sleeping while the church prayed for him. And when he came to himself, what did he realize?

4. How and why did Herod die?

5. Explain the separation of Paul and Barnabas, and who did Paul choose to teach and preach with him, after the separation?

6. Paul was "long winded" when he preached. What happened to Eutychus during one of these sessions?

7. On the island called Melita, Paul was bitten by a viper. What harm came to him and how did the Barbarians react to this incident?

8. Upon Paul's arrival in Rome, he called the chief of the Jews together. And when they had appointed him a day to preach/teach, what were the turn of events?

THE END – ESSAY – THE NEW TESTAMENT

ANSWERS ONLY TO THE OLD TESTAMENT ESSAYS (AO)
GENESIS - SIX (6) ESSAY AO

1. GENESIS CHAPTERS 1- 3
2. GENESIS CHAPTER 4
3. GENESIS 6:3-16 AND GENESIS 7:24
4. GENESIS 16: 1 AND 4   GENESIS 16:10-11
5. GENESIS 25: 24-26
    GENESIS 27: 36 AND 41
    GENESIS 29: 1-26
    GENESIS 31: 1-20
6. GENESIS 30: 23-24
    GENESIS CHAPTER 37 TO CHAPTER 50

EXODUS – THREE (3) ESSAY AO
1. EXODUS 2:5-6
2. (1) ROD TO A SERPENT   (2) RIVER WATER BECAME BLOOD
    (3) FROGS   (4) LICE   (5) SWARMS OF FLIES   (6) BOILS
    (7) ASHES BECOME DUST   (8) GRIEVOUS RAIL/HAIL
    (9) LOCUSTS   (10) PLAGUE OF DARKNESS
3. EXODUS 20:3-17

LEVITICUS – THREE (3) ESSAY AO
1. LEVITICUS 10:1-3
2. LEVITICUS CHAPTER 26
3. LEVITICUS 27:32

NUMBERS – FIVE (5) AO
1. NUMBERS 1:53
2. NUMBERS CHAPTER 6
3. NUMBERS CHAPTER 12
4. NUMBERS 18:24-26
5. NUMBERS 27:12-23

DEUTERONOMY – TRREE (3) AO
1. DEUTERONOMY 5:1-22
2. DEUTERONOMY CHAPTER 28
3. DEUTERONOMY 34:4-9

THE END – AO – OLD TESTAMENT

THE ANSWERS ONLY TO THE NEW TESTAMENT ESSAYS (AO)

ST. MATTHEW - FIVE (5) ESSAY AO
1. MATTHEW CHAPTER 3
2. MATTHEW 13:18-30
3. MATTHEW 15:13-20
4. MATTHEW 9:18-22
   MATTHEWS 9;27-30
   MATTHEW 14:25-32
5. MATTHEW 28:16-20

ST. MARK - FIVE (5) ESSAY AO
1. MARK 3:14-18
2. MARK 3:29
3. MARK 9:29
4. MARK 14:43-44
   MARK 14:68
   MARK 14:70-71
5. MARK 15:17

ST. LUKE - SIX (6) ESSAY AO
1. LUKE 1:11
   LUKE 1:19-20
2. LUKE 2:7-16
3. LUKE 4:17-19
4. LUKE 9:1-5
5. LUKE 15:11-32
6. LUKE 24: 45-49

ST. JOHN - SEVEN (7) ESSAY AO
1. JOHN 1:14-23
2. JOHN 8:6-18
3. JOHN 11:35
4. JOHN 13:21-27
5. JOHN 19:17-20
6. JOHN 19:23-24
7. JOHN 20:24
   JOHN 20:27

THE ACTS - EIGHT (8) ESSAY AO
1. ACTS 9:1-21
   ACTS 13:9
2. ACTS 11:5-9
3. ACTS 12:11
4. ACTS 12:23

5. ACTS 15:35-40
6. ACTS 20:9-12
7. ACTS 28:3-6
8. ACTS 28:23-31

THE END – ESSAY AO – THE NEW TESTAMENT